"You're loo̶̶̶̶̶ ̶ ̶ ̶ ̶ me..."

Hell, Stella wanted to do a lot more than touch. In her mind, the image flashed of her fingers on the button of Owen's jeans and working down the fly. A memory? No, more like wishful thinking. Because that was what she would have done last night. And after she'd slid the zipper down she would have shoved the soft material down his hips just far enough to free him. She'd lick his collarbone. Nip his skin with her teeth. Trail her tongue down his body until she reached his—

"Don't do that," he gritted out. "I'm doing everything I can to not lift you onto my shoulder, carry you into that bedroom and make up for what I don't remember."

"Owen, I—"

He squeezed his eyes shut. "Don't say my name. You say it like a moan. Don't look at me like you want my hands all over your body." He gripped her shoulders and his gaze locked with hers. Hunger blazed in those hazel depths. Hunger for her.

"I want you. But not like this..."

Dear Reader,

I've done my fair share of odd things in the name of volunteering, from being dunked in ice-cold water to participating in a rum study. But never once have I woken up in handcuffs (yet)! Of course, a lot worse happens to Stella and Owen, but really, they only have themselves to blame.

I had a blast writing this story about this soon-to-be doctor and a smoke jumper, and it's not because I had to look at a lot of pictures on the internet of sexy firemen doing their job. Although I'm truly humbled by the amazing work all first responders and our medical professionals take on every day at all hours. I loved writing the sizzling connection and unexpected attraction between Stella and Owen. They weren't prepared for love, but had to adapt—stat!

It was also fun to catch up with Larissa and her long-term crush, Dr. Mitch Durant, as well as the other couple they send on a winding happily-ever-after path—Hayden Taylor and Anthony Garcia. If you'd like to read Hayden and Tony's story, check out *Naked Thrill*.

I can be found hanging around my website, jillmonroe.com—handcuffs optional!

Best,

Jill

Jill Monroe

Naked Pursuit

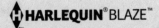
HARLEQUIN® BLAZE™

Recycling programs
for this product may
not exist in your area.

ISBN-13: 978-0-373-79886-5

Naked Pursuit

Printed in U.S.A.

Jill Monroe makes her home in Oklahoma with her family. When not writing, she spends way too much time on the internet completing "research" or updating her blog. Even when writing, she's thinking of ways to avoid cooking.

Books by Jill Monroe

Harlequin Blaze

Share the Darkness
Hitting the Mark
Tall, Dark and Filthy Rich
Primal Instincts
Wet and Wild
SEALed and Delivered
SEALed with a Kiss
Naked Thrill

Harlequin Nocturne

Lord of Rage

As always, this book is dedicated to my family.

Thanks go to Gena Showalter, Candace Havens, Allison Kent, HelenKay Dimon, Stephanie Feagan, Wendy Duren and never last (except in this list) Kassia Krozser.

Special thanks to Deidre Knight and Adrienne Macintosh—you ladies rock!

Prologue

"YOU CAN'T LEAVE," Larissa Winston said as she gripped the wood molding lining the doorway, blocking the exit from the patient lounge into the lobby with her body.

Was she really doing this? When had jamming herself between the door and the hallway become part of her job description at PharmaTest?

Four faces stared back at her, each one reflecting a different response: wildness, humor, recklessness and utter disorder. None of which she'd seen in previous test subjects.

Under the watchful eye of the amazing Dr. Mitch Durant, the drug HB121 had been in clinical trials for nearly a year. Usually the test patients simply went to their bunks and quietly slept the night away. In the morning, Larissa would ask a few exit questions, take the subjects' vitals and process the paperwork for payment. Easy-peasy.

There had never, not one time, ever been a patient revolt. Until now.

She manufactured a stern voice, a combination of the voices of her mother and that scary teacher she'd had in the second grade. "If you will all please return to the patient lounge, I can get you something to eat. I'm sure you'll be getting very tired soon. I have assigned you each a room for you to rest in until morning. Why don't you—"

"Are you preventing us from leaving?" the pretty young brunette asked, subject number thirty-five.

"This should make for a very interesting angle to my film," test subject seventy-eight informed Larissa as he lifted his phone and aimed the camera lens in her direction. Ah yes, this volunteer was the California documentary filmmaker. "Please confess to the world how PharmaTest kidnaps patients and holds them here at the testing center in Dallas, Texas, against their will."

"Yeah," the pretty brunette at his side cheered him on. Were they together now? Already?

Larissa had distributed the testing dose to each of them less than an hour ago. How were people coupling up? They should be in deep REM by now, in that dreamless sleep of the fully medicated.

But the filmmaker's threat hung heavy in the air. A sudden wave of panic struck her in the stomach. Larissa was no social-media dummy. This video would go viral. In less than a second, her Twitter handle would spread from one tweet to the next, followed by the public shaming and embarrassing meme, finally culminating in job loss. If she was lucky.

She plastered on a smile and lowered her arms. "Of course I'm not trying to kidnap you. I have some tea, or perhaps you'd prefer some flavored water? Let's go to the lounge and you can choose. It's all part of the compensation for your time. As well as the money you're being *paid* as a *volunteer* test subject."

"You can keep the forty bucks," offered the firefighter from Colorado.

That man was delicious, all rugged and well-honed

muscles. Not exactly her type, though. Larissa's weakness was the smart-with-glasses, quiet, sciencey type, like Dr. Mitch Durant. He was the head researcher on this study and the reason she'd stuck around on a job for which the hours were from eight at night until seven in the morning, often screwing up her weekends.

The med student—uh…Stella Holbrook—hooked her hand around the firefighter's arm. Wait, was this another quickie pairing? Had Dr. Mitch tweaked with the formula again? Added some kind of hooking-up pheromone? Not that she blamed the woman for being intrigued with the firefighter, but c'mon, ladies and gents. This was an experimental drug test, not the club.

Larissa couldn't just let them leave, could she?

Of course, the four of them were all adults. They could make their own choices. But more importantly, they'd all been required to sign waivers releasing PharmaTest from any liability. Larissa would never have distributed the meds without double-checking to make sure that important detail had been taken care of.

But her dilemma wasn't just the patients' well-being. Dr. Durant's research was important, not just to the man who'd put every bit of himself and his career into developing HB121, but also to the potential pain it would prevent for the hurt and wounded of the world, allowing doctors to give life-saving aid. How many times had Dr. Mitch gifted her with the smile that reached all the way to his dark eyes and told her how important she was to his team? Even now a tiny little thrill inched its way down her vertebrae at the memory. Larissa had to fix this situation for him. *Now.*

Clearly the pacifying approach wasn't working. The four looked like they'd rush her at any moment. And they'd win. At five foot two, she'd always been shorter than everyone else on the playground. She'd hated Red Rover.

Maybe a play on their altruistic side would do the trick. "This research is important. All of you wanted to do something to further this study. To help people. By leaving now, you're changing the sample. That will make the conclusions and results suspect."

"You said we should be sleeping, right?" the med student asked, a line forming between her brows.

"The drug is designed so that the patient can answer questions if needed or even respond to stimuli and move if in danger, but yes, for the most part, the injured is unconscious." Larissa nodded, a wave of relief allowing her to breathe again. She was getting through. Finally. At least to the med student. Maybe if Larissa could get her to understand, then the soon-to-be Dr. Holbrook would help to convince the others to stay until their portion of the study was completed in the morning.

"Then, since we're not asleep, we must be in the control group that got a placebo," the future doc said, the line on her forehead gone and a smile on her lips.

Subject thirty-five nodded. "I've done enough drug trials to know that's true. I think we can go without changing the end results. You can keep my money, too."

"What if you're not in the control group? Please listen to me. This medication is designed to take away fear and panic. Think about it. Are you acting rationally? You'd planned to stay the night as test subjects, and suddenly you want to leave..." Larissa let her words trail off so the significance of what she was saying would sink in with the four of them.

"We're leaving because this place blows."

"Big time."

"I'm ready to do something fun for a change."

Their words came at her fast and furious. She'd lost. Larissa's shoulders slumped.

In the future she'd probably end the retelling of this story with, "And that's how I lost my job…"

And how she lost the man she so, so wanted to see naked. Just once.

But she could still protect him and his research. She owed Dr. Durant that. The kind of people who gave research grants tended to shy away from scandal, and Mitch needed the funding to continue with his work.

"I'm going to ask you to sign something, stating you are leaving the study early and on your own. That you don't hold me or PharmaTest liable and you don't expect to be compensated for your time."

"Why?" the filmmaker asked.

"Because, Mr. Garcia, one of the side effects is short-term memory loss. Usually for twenty-four hours. Still interested in leaving?"

"Oh, we're leaving," Mr. Garcia said, and the others nodded.

1

STELLA RAN OUT into the night, Owen right beside her. Hayden and Tony were close on their heels. "I thought that lady was never going to let us leave," she said as they slowed outside the PharmaTest front door.

"Good idea about the camera, Tony," Hayden told him, her smile wide in the fading daylight.

The man fell deeper under her spell, not that he appeared to want to stop himself. "That will be the last time I walk into someplace on the spur of the moment. But then, if I hadn't, I wouldn't be here with you now. And that's something I would regret," he told her, his voice soft and intimate.

Normally something that sweet would make Stella give a mock shudder and say something snarky, like "bring out the chips for that cheese." But one look at the tender and serious expression on Tony's face, and anyone could see he meant exactly what he'd said. It was charming how this tough guy caught her off guard and slipped under her defenses.

Hayden's whole body angled toward Tony. Oh, yeah, she was a goner.

Stella's gaze slid away from the couple and smacked

straight into Owen's. His intent hazel eyes were focused solely on her, and Stella's breath stilled. Everything stilled. Hayden's and Tony's soft words faded, the strong Texas wind dwindled, and it was just the two of them, searching for something in each other's eyes.

Okay, sure, those were some pretty over-the-top observations, but this was a very over-the-top moment for her. As a medical student, she worked in fact and science. Feelings rarely counted. They couldn't. But tonight, she wanted to let emotions and feelings and passion blow right past sensibility. She could allow herself that. For tonight.

Only two steps separated her from the wall of his chest. She took those two steps in a heady rush, lifted herself on her toes and brushed her lips across his. Soft and quick. Once. Twice. Testing the waters.

Her heels hit the pavement, and she stared at Owen for a moment.

Plunge right in. The water's fine.

She lifted on the tips of her toes again, ready to explore this sexy man fully. His hands circled around her hips, and his head lowered—

"Let's get out of here before clipboard lady comes back," Tony interrupted. "I'll pull my car around."

"That was just getting interesting," Owen said, and smiled down at her, his gaze straying to her lips for a brief second, then returning to her eyes.

She met his smile and nodded.

He lifted a brow. "You want to get out of here? Actually, wait here. I'll go with Tony to get his car. If you change your mind and you're gone when we come back, I'll understand. But—"

Owen interrupted his own words by lowering his head and settling his lips on hers. Whereas her kisses had been

quick explorations, his kiss was all about sweet persua-
sion. He traced her upper lip with his tongue, then gently tugged her lower lip into the warmth of his mouth.

She was ready for something more. So much more.

He cupped her cheeks with his hands and slid his
tongue into her mouth. Owen urged her to meet his kiss
with equal passion, and by his slow, anguished groan,
she accomplished just that. His heat surrounded her. His
woodsy scent filled her nose. Her nipples hardened and
puckered against the soft silk of her bra.

"C'mon, Owen," Tony called.

"I hope you're here when I come back," he whispered
against her lips, and then he was walking away from her.

She wasn't usually the kind of lady to ogle a guy's
backside. To her, a body wasn't something to gawk at but
to examine and study and, on good days, to be amazed
by. She loved learning about all the wonderful and incredible things the human body could accomplish, from
bringing forth new life to running a marathon to over-
coming invasive surgery and disease. Really, a leg was
a leg and a chest was a chest.

But with Owen, it was different. She could appreciate
the tight package of his ass. Or the roped, caged strength
of his arms as he'd held her. And Stella had to laugh at
herself because she wanted to examine Owen, all right,
just not in the medical sense. Cue the jokes about play-
ing doctor. She raised her arms above her head and spun,
laughing and squeezing her eyes shut tight. The heavy
night air welcomed her.

"Are you actually...twirling?" Hayden asked her.

Stella slowed until she was just moving with a slight
sway and glanced over to her fellow escapee. Hayden,
also known as her new best friend, frowned at her.

"I don't think I've ever been happy enough to twirl.

Or spin. At least not since I was six. That's kind of sad. What happens to us that we don't want to spin anymore?"

Hayden shrugged. "Life, I guess. I was kind of judgey about your spinning a second ago, but now I'm going to join you because we *should* spin."

And for one perfect moment, they circled in the parking lot, laughing and reconnecting to their six-year-old selves who'd thought—no, *knew*—that twirling was perfectly acceptable. Even preferred.

"I'm getting a little dizzy," Stella said. She planted her feet on the concrete until the world around her slowed. Adulthood always snuck in somehow.

"I can't believe I left the study like that. I have always, *always* done what I was supposed to do," Hayden confided.

"Good for you, then. In fact, you should keep breaking the rules tonight."

"What?" Tony said from behind them. His navy sports car was parked on the street. Owen unfolded his tall frame from the passenger seat and smiled at her. Yep, an onslaught of goofy responses predictably followed.

"Tonight Hayden should do everything she's not supposed to." Tony lifted a brow, acute interest practically radiating from the man. She was happy for her friend that this cute guy was so into her. Tony laced Hayden's fingers through his.

"Cool car. Does the top go down?" she asked as the two of them walked together toward his car.

"And what about you?" Owen asked Stella. "What do you want to do tonight?"

Her skin prickled and sweat broke out on the back of her neck. So this delicious warmth spreading through her was what *it* felt like. Because if she wasn't mistaken, at this very moment, Stella was the subject of some acute male interest, too. And while Tony was great and all, there was a recklessness about Owen, the kind of wink-at-danger swagger and bring-it-on attitude that made her sit up straight and say "yes, please."

Factor in his sinfully sexy smile and perfectly muscled body, and she was a goner.

You. I want to do you. But it was more than that...

"Tonight I'm living life," she stated. "I'm not going to watch it from the sidelines. I'm going to grab it, feel it and give it a good shake. You see, right now I want to kiss you again, and that's something I never would have done before, and I certainly never would have told you about it. Because kissing a man can lead to way too many feelings and emotions, and I have to keep that kind of stuff contained in order to succeed."

"Who told you that?" he challenged.

"Learned it from the best—my parents. I've seen way too many people alter their perfectly arranged paths because of sex and relationships. But not me. Never me. My plans—degree, med school, ER, end of story."

"So what do you do when something, or someone, threatens all that perfect planning?" His fingers traced down her arm, diverting her train of thought.

"I slow it down and console myself that if it's meant to be, it will be. Only later." Stella held her breath for a moment. Swallowed. "But with you, I want to *make* it be. Right. Now."

He crooked his elbow toward her. "Coming with me, then?"

"Absolutely."

Arm-in-arm, they dove into the backseat of Tony's car like two stars escaping from the paparazzi. She wound up across his lap, her legs tangled with his. And as the sun set outside their window and the dark enveloped them, she twined her fingers behind Owen's neck and his lips found hers.

"Tony, that's it," Hayden said from the front seat.

Owen's lips left hers before their lip-lock could really get started. He kissed her temple instead. "Didn't take long for them to interrupt. What was that, fifteen seconds?" He grumbled against the sensitive skin of her neck and she giggled.

"Shorter." Too short. Stella straightened in the seat and pushed what had to be her very unruly hair from her face. She glanced out the window to find out what Hayden was so excited about. "What's *it*?" she finally asked, because all she saw were nondescript office buildings and parking lots.

"The first thing I'm not supposed to do," Hayden said, pointing to her right.

Tony slowed and angled the car in front of a long aluminum building with a you-could-see-it-from-anywhere neon sign of a roller skate, flashing in bright green and blue. How had Stella missed that blinding splash of color?

"You're not supposed to roller-skate?" she asked. Stella could come up with half a dozen medical reasons a young woman of reasonable health shouldn't skate, but none of them visibly applied to Hayden.

"Well, it was a long time ago, but my grandparents had some definite ideas of the kind of trouble a girl could get herself into in the darkened corners of a roller rink."

Now that made sense. "All my preteen angst just came flooding back," Stella admitted, awash in fond memories. When makeup was experimental (and forbidden) and her best friend had taught her how to practice kissing on her hand at a slumber party. Everything had seemed so important and boys too complicated.

Actually, not much had changed. Well, except for to-

night. This thing with Owen felt anything but complicated, and the only important plan was to live this night
fully.

"Girls used to whisper and brag how they made out
at the roller rink at school," Hayden confided, her tone
a little wistful. She opened the door, and the overhead
light popped on, making her blink.

Tony lifted a brow. "You didn't?" he asked her.

She rolled her eyes. "As if my grandparents would
ever have permitted that."

He rushed around the car and met her at the door, offering his hand to her like a gallant knight. "Allow me
to change that."

"Absolutely," she said, and reached her fingers toward
his.

"What about you, Stella? Was kissing at the rink part
of your education?" Owen asked as they scrambled out
of the car to stand on the sidewalk.

"Maybe," she hedged.

Actually, it hadn't. At a party, she'd been dared to
kiss the guy she'd been crushing on and she'd planted
the worst kiss in the history of worst kisses on the guy.
She'd missed his lips and managed to swipe the side of his
nose instead. He'd rolled away to laugh about her with his
friends, and she'd ended up borrowing a stranger's phone
to call her mom to pick her up from the party early. That
was Stella's first official lesson in keeping her emotions
to herself, and boys at a distance.

Beside her, Owen crooked his elbow in a gentlemanly
move that she was beginning to recognize as his signa-
ture. "Let's make it not a maybe," he said.

But maybe she could forget that lesson. At least for
the night. With a nod, she hooked her arm through his
and they walked inside together. She kind of enjoyed this

linking elbows thing they had going. As if they were a team ready to face danger or fun together. Probably both.

The familiar scents of perfume and cologne and the oil used on the wooden floor of the roller rink made her stomach clench for a moment. Her most embarrassing experience had happened at a place just like this, and she preferred not to dwell on emotions that brought her down. The roller rink had never figured into any of her plans past the age of fourteen.

But she also smelled beer and gourmet pretzels. Patrons leaned against the railing surrounding the rink while sipping on martinis and gin and tonics, not sodas and fruit punch. Owen wasn't some teenage boy interested in looking cool to his friends. And Stella definitely knew how to kiss a man now. Besides, she was all about living life tonight, not avoiding it. Roller-skating it was.

They joined Tony and Hayden in the lobby of the rink, where the pair was waiting in line.

Hayden greeted her with a smile. "Stella, it's adult skate night. It's like this night was tailor-made for us."

Tony pulled out his cell phone and they laughed and posed for selfies.

"This light is doing weird things to your hair," Hayden said. "First pink. Then blue."

Stella fluffed her curly locks. "Try to catch one when I look blond."

Finally it was their turn at the register. The guys paid the admission, and the four of them exchanged shoes for skates.

The music pumped, a combination of disco from the seventies, new wave from the eighties and bubblegum pop from the nineties. Their skin was awash in silver patterns from the mirrored balls above their heads and the pulsing strobe lights suspended from the ceiling.

They sat on one of the long carpeted benches that lined the skating area and put on their skates. Hayden and Tony quickly laced up, but Stella's pace was slower so she could take this night all in. She didn't allow herself to break out of her self-restraint that often, so she wanted to really live this moment—the sound of the music and the laughing couples around them, the thump of the bass beneath her socked feet and the steady warmth of Owen's shoulder as he sat beside her.

Hayden gave her a wink as they skated off, and in moments Stella lost the other couple in the crowd on the hardwood roller floor.

Owen didn't seem to be in much of a hurry, either. She snuck a peek at his profile. He looked pensive. "Everything okay?" she asked over the din of the music.

He angled toward her and flashed her that amazing smile of his. The one she'd first noticed in the Pharma-Test waiting room when it had triggered some secret little voice inside her mind that said *exactly*.

"I'm thinking that the moment I get out on that floor in my skates, any chance of looking cool and impressing the lady I want is definitely out."

Stella couldn't help but laugh. This sexy hunk of a man wanted to impress her, and that made something inside her go all gooey toward him.

The prospect of her carefully honed defenses crumbling should have scared the hell out of her. Her parents had insisted she'd need a tough shell in order to have a life as an ER doctor, so she'd guarded herself from emotion for as long as she could remember.

But tonight she craved more. Her usual choice of guy leaned to the nerdier type—the kind of man who didn't worry so much about appearing cool because he was so far away from that descriptor anyway.

With his wide shoulders and strong arms, Owen probably played sports. His easy confidence around her—and, well, everyone—suggested he was the guy who'd always been invited to the popular parties in high school. The kind of guy who saw through girls like her. But not tonight. Owen wanted her, and he wasn't afraid of saying it or showing it.

Maybe he deserved some honesty from her. "But if you don't go out on that floor, how will I ever be able to pretend to fall so that you can catch me?" she asked.

The smile dropped from his lips, and in a flash of strobe lighting she caught the intensity of his gaze. Just for a moment. Then the light moved and he was concealed once more.

His thumb stroked the back of her hand and tiny shivers spread through her fingers and down her arm. Imagine what she'd feel if that thumb stroked other needy places on her body? And *that* naughty little thought brought on a full body quake.

"What was that fantasy about darkened corners Hayden mentioned?"

Stella swiveled on the bench, searching for someplace private where she could replace her teenage roller-skating failure with a warm memory of kissing the hunky guy. *Finally.* The kind of memory she could think about while on those rough twelve-hour shifts that awaited her in the emergency room.

Another beam of light flashed across his face, and she caught a teasing glint in his eyes. He leaned in to whisper in her ear. "Just to warn you, I'm about to throw down the worst line. Ready?"

Was she? Absolut— *Wait a minute, don't just sit there and passively let this smooth, gorgeous man lay down the moves. This is your night to live. Live it.* She gave him the side eye. "It's not the one about guessing the material of your shirt and it turns out to be boyfriend material, is it?"

He scratched at his chin. "That's pretty good, and by *good* I mean *terrible*. But actually, I can do worse. Much worse," he assured her.

She pretended to shake out her muscles and roll her shoulders like a swimmer readying for the block. "Okay, I'm ready."

"When I saw you at PharmaTest earlier tonight, I knew there was no way I'd leave before finding out if your personality was as amazing as your smile."

Her mouth dried, and she had a hard time swallowing for a moment. "That really wasn't a bad line," she confessed, her words rushing out on an abrupt exhalation. She'd expected some kind of teasing comment, and instead he'd dropped the mother of all flirtbombs.

"Worth that darkened corner?" he asked.

The skates slipped from her fingers as she stood. "Oh, yeah. I spotted one, right there by the lockers." Although truth be told, he didn't need a line. Stella had wanted to kiss Owen since he'd caught her eye when they'd been filling out the paperwork at PharmaTest. Surely he knew that.

Her heartbeat pounded as they threaded between the people around the rink, seeking the dim nook she'd discovered earlier, perfect for making out. All their other kisses had been spontaneous, moments of daring with no forethought at all. But this next kiss would be deliberate and purposeful. And because of that, this moment felt more important.

She pulled him into the corner and leaned against the smooth wall of painted cinderblock, the coolness seeping into her overheated skin through the thin layer of her shirt. Owen braced his weight on his arm above her head.

His gaze moved to her mouth, and a half smile flickered on his lips that quickly changed to an intense hunger.

Yes. She wanted to feel that. *Exactly* that. He gently stroked her lower lip with his thumb, and her eyes drifted shut for a moment so she could savor how he made her respond. Her blood heated in her veins and anticipation rushed through her. She drew the tip of his thumb into her mouth and he groaned. The harsh sound made her body tremble.

Never had she responded to a man like this. Never had her body craved a man's caress on her skin so much. Stella hungered for his mouth, his taste.

"I feel like I'm losing my mind over you."

The raw wonder in his voice triggered a deep yearning inside her. Her knees grew a little shaky and warmth flooded between her legs.

"You're not the only one," she admitted, her voice unsteady, and he graced her with that brief half smile again.

Stella reached for him. Her fingers curled into the muscles of his shoulders and urged him closer. He lowered his mouth to hers. It was the barest of strokes, and yet she shivered from that too-slight caress. She breathed in his intoxicating scent as her eyes closed. She locked her hands behind Owen's neck, his short hair tickling the backs of her fingers. He continued his sensual light exploration of her mouth then *finally* his tongue traced the seam of her lips.

Stella gasped at the sweet sensation, and then his tongue twined with hers. *Exactly.*

If fourteen-year-old her had experienced the worst liplock at a place like this, the twenty-five-year-old Stella was wiping that memory away for good with this incredible, mind-boggling kiss. This time her lips found their target and she pressed her body against the strength of his chest, her nipples tingling inside the restrictive cups of her bra. She breathed and tasted and felt only Owen. Reveled in the sensations spiraling and building inside her.

A shrill whistle sounded near her ear. And not the silly, exaggerated I-caught-you-making-out kind of whistle. But the teacher-telling-you-to-stop-throwing-dirt-on-the-playground screech that sent a wave of panic through her system even now that she was an adult. Stella broke her kiss-tender lips from his and forced her eyes open.

She had to squint and blink a few times before the picture in front of her eyes righted itself. A man sporting a black-and-white-striped referee shirt skated toward them and waved his hands. The suspect whistle hung around his neck, suspended from a lanyard.

He slid to a stop beside them. "You can't do *that* in here. This is a family place." He emphasized the word with a disgusted shake of his hand.

"It's adult skate night," Owen said after glancing around to confirm that no children had magically appeared in the rink. They'd shared a harmless kiss in the shadows of a darkened corner.

"This isn't my first lap around the rink," the referee said. "I know what comes next."

Yeah, she did, too. Not that either of them would have indulged in such a public place. Then again, how long before her hands found that sweet curve of his ass? Or his fingers toyed with her nipples? Her breasts grew heavy at just the thought of him palming her so intimately.

"Uh, Owen. I don't want to skate anymore."

His gaze lowered to hers, his eyes searching in the dark. He must have sensed the sexual cravings that battered her senses, because his spine abruptly straightened and he cleared his throat. Twice.

"Neither do I." His voice was a whispered promise,

and a shiver shimmied between her shoulder blades and settled in the small of her back. Then he focused his attention to the ref. "Sorry if we disturbed anyone. We're leaving."

Yeah, she couldn't wait to be alone with this sexy man. Owen laced his fingers through hers and they moved away, the echo of the ref's wheels on the floor sounding behind them as he returned to the rink. "Hate adult skate," he mumbled.

"Tony," Owen called, finding Tony and Hayden nearly hidden by a row of lockers a few rows away from them.

"Careful, you two," Stella teased. "There's a no-kissing policy here."

"Found that out a moment ago ourselves," Hayden told her, smiling.

"We're going to exchange our shoes," Tony said, and Owen winked at Stella before he left, causing a shaft of awareness down her back.

Beside her, Hayden seemed to be experiencing her own struggles because the woman couldn't focus on anything but Tony's backside as the two men walked away.

"Good for you," Stella told her.

Hayden nodded. "Yeah, it is good. I've been working so hard lately, I needed a bit of distraction," she confessed, her gaze once again straying over to Tony.

"I know what you mean. Everyone always says how rough the third year of med school is on a person, but I guess I hadn't realized just how much of a toll it was taking on me until tonight, when I finally relaxed. I don't think the tension has left my body in two and a half years."

"Well, tonight I plan to get all tense, then relax. Then tense all up again." Hayden wiped a hand over her face. "Oh, I make such terrible jokes sometimes."

But the two of them began to laugh. Hell, Stella had just been discovered making out like an errant teenager at a school dance, but instead of feeling mortified, she was giggling with a near stranger, and it felt great. Really great.

Tony reached for Hayden's hand just as Owen draped an arm around her shoulders. And that felt even better.

"I don't know whether to be relieved or frightened to find two women laughing," Owen teased.

"Oh, it's both," Stella assured him, trying to insert every sexy tone she'd ever heard in a movie straight into her voice.

Must have worked, because the smile faded from Owen's face. "See you guys later," he said, not even bothering to look away from her to address Hayden and Tony.

Hayden gave her the thumbs-up.

After stopping only to put on their shoes, they fled the rink like two teenagers who'd snuck out of the house without being caught. The cool night air caressed her skin as they stepped outside.

"You don't mind walking back to the car instead of waiting on Tony and Hayden? I doubt we got too far from PharmaTest."

But who was to know since they'd spent the entire ride in the backseat in each other's arms? Stella shook her head; a little night air would do her good.

"How'd you end up at PharmaTest?" he asked, matching the length of his stride to hers as they walked. He draped his arm around her shoulders again; the heat from his body warmed her.

"I volunteer for a lot of medical studies, or at least I used to. I'm in med school now, so I don't have much time. But since it's fall break and this was an overnight trial, I thought I could fit it in. What about you?" she asked.

"I knew someone."

That's all he needed to say. At some point in his life, Owen had lost a friend. It struck her as something special that he cared enough to try to make sure others *did* make it to see another day. "That's the real reason doctors do what we do. To help others."

This wasn't just a guy she could take to bed and leave all emotion behind. Owen was a man she could actually like. Which made him not the best candidate for a one-off night of ecstasy, but she wasn't backing away now. Owen was the man she wanted.

"Where to?" he asked when they were alone in the PharmaTest parking lot. He'd been right; they had traveled only a few blocks in Tony's sports car. "You want to find someplace else to go? Wanna grab something to eat?"

But Stella didn't want to talk or think. "What do you want to do?" she asked, knowing he wasn't the kind of man for delay tactics. He'd made it clear he wanted her, and right now she wanted to hear it. Again.

He gifted her with that sexy half smile again. "I don't care what we do. Or where we go. I just want to be with you."

Exactly. She just wanted to kiss this gorgeous, sexy man again and again. She sank her fingers into the short hair behind his neck and urged his lips toward hers.

Not much urging was required. With a groan, his lips once again settled against hers. "I've thought of nothing else since spotting you at this place," he admitted against her mouth. Then his tongue slipped inside her mouth and along her tongue and she was done. Done in. Done for. Exactly what the doctor ordered.

Seriously? What the doctor ordered? Had she just made that crack in her head? So Hayden wasn't the only one who could make bad jokes.

Time to get serious. "Your place close?" she asked between kisses.

He cupped her face, stroking her cheeks with the pads of his thumbs. His eyes were heavy-lidded with desire, his hazel eyes almost brown. "I don't live in Dallas. I'm only here a few days, visiting for my grandmother's birthday, and the place is too crowded. You?"

She shook her head. "Same. I have three roommates."

"I want to be alone with you," he said, the warmth of his breath teasing her temple.

Had this guy actually made her shiver with just a few whispered words? Him. *Exactly.*

"Alone with you sounds about perfect."

His eyes squeezed shut for a moment, and a small smile played along his lips. Had he doubted how much she wanted him? Well, yeah, probably, because when did this kind of devastating instawant actually happen? His show of relief made warmth spread throughout her body.

His hazel eyes opened and his smile widened. For her. "It's been a while since I've been in Dallas, but I think there's a hotel not far from here."

Stella nodded. "I know the one. By the park."

"My car's that way," he told her, pointing toward a battered truck with Colorado plates. They raced together toward his car.

The hotel was far swankier than she'd remembered. A landmark boutique hotel in the Dallas area, it had a lush art-deco lobby, complete with a large crackling fire. The rubber soles of her shoes didn't do justice to the sleek hardwood floors beneath them, set in striking geometric designs. Chevron-patterned wallpaper lined the walls.

Thick, luxurious drapes in gold and burgundy flanked the deep-set bay windows, many of them displaying stained glass that she would have loved to inspect—if she weren't with the world's sexiest man.

Everything about the place screamed luxury and expense. Except a place like this didn't scream. Never anything that crass. This was the hotel that enforced a dress code, and while Owen looked amazing in his jeans and casual polo shirt, his clothes were not fit for the Market Gardens hotel. Or hers.

But Owen kept walking to the ornately carved wooden desk that was less like a check-in counter and more like the kind of thing a millionaire shipping tycoon—no, a billionaire investment banker—kicked up her stilettos on.

"Welcome to the Market Gardens. What name is your reservation under?" the friendly yet cool clerk asked them. In a suit and tie, he looked exactly like the kind of man who could hold his own against the wealthily entitled of the world as well as two people who'd just walked in off the street on a whim.

Stella bit back a laugh. They'd not thought this hotel plan through. Of course the Market Gardens required reservations. She began to turn away.

But Owen played it cool as well, which probably wasn't a stretch for him. "No reservation. What do you have available?"

The smile faded from the clerk's face. "We're usually booked up several weeks in advance."

They must look like exactly what they were—two people up for a little spontaneous rendezvous. Even that was too generous. Sex. They were down for some hot and dirty sex.

"We're only interested in tonight," Owen continued. With lips pursed, the clerk toggled the mouse and woke up the computer discreetly hidden beneath a carved wood panel.

"Would you prefer a courtyard view?" he asked. "I have a suite."

Her shoulders stiffened in alarm. A courtyard view in this place must cost a fortune. "That's okay—"

"Absolutely," Owen said, and slid his credit card toward the reservationist.

"You'll be in one of our tower rooms, second floor." With a few clicks of the mouse and a swipe of the card, the transaction was complete. The clerk slid over a leather case containing their key cards.

Wow. Even the fanciest hotel she'd ever stayed at had only presented her with a folded-over piece of cardstock with the plastic key card stuffed inside.

The clerk signaled for the bellhop. A young man sporting a gray blazer trimmed with gold at the cuff and neck quickly appeared, friendly smile in place.

"We don't have any luggage," Owen informed them without a trace of embarrassment, even though she felt the heat of a blush in her cheeks.

"Of course, sir," the clerk responded coolly, unfazed.

Why should she even care? She was here to live her life before her job took it over again after this quick break.

"Actually, I do have a duffel bag inside my truck. I'll be right back."

No way was he leaving her here alone in the lobby of snobs. Stella quickly followed on his heels.

He'd mentioned earlier that he'd wanted to impress her. She didn't want him to face an ugly credit card bill to do it. "Owen, this place has got to be way too much money."

"It's on me," he told her and fished out the keys to his truck. A large black duffel bag rested on the backseat, and he picked it up and swung it up over his shoulder.

Stella had grown up with two working doctors for parents, so money had never been tight, but rash expensive impulses weren't something they'd ever indulged in. She didn't want Owen to feel as if she expected it. "I just don't want you to think you have to spend a lot of money on me. Maybe they have another roo—"

He gripped her by the shoulders. "Stella, it's done. The only excuse my parents would accept for me not staying with them is that I'm at the Market Gardens. Besides, we're living life," he told her, then stifled any further protest with a kiss.

Living life in a swanky hotel with the world's sexiest guy…why was she complaining again? He crooked his elbow to her in the habit of his that she was really beginning to like.

"The elevator is right this way," the bellman informed them as they entered. They followed him into one of the elevators. She met Owen's gaze on the short trip to the second floor. Heat and desire emanated from his gaze. It was amazing to be wanted so desperately.

The bell dinged above their heads but didn't break the spell between them. With each step toward their room, her body ached more and more with yearning. She needed this man's hands on her skin. His lips teasing her nipples. His fingers between her legs.

The bellman swept the door wide, and she gasped at the lavish room. She'd heard the word *suite* when the clerk had confirmed the reservation, but Owen had booked a Suite with a capital *S*.

A beautiful sitting area beckoned them to indulge in luxury. A small two-person dinette waited for them in the corner, decorated with a vase of fresh Texas wildflowers. Her feet sank into the thick carpet, but she forced herself not to rush toward the bedroom. Slow and steady steps would get her there just the same.

Owen tipped the bellman and followed her into the bedroom.

"Is there a bigger bed size than king?" she asked. "I think an entire family could sleep on this—"

He cut off her musings by tracing the curve of her ear with his tongue. Her eyes drifted shut and she leaned against him. Her back fit perfectly against his chest.

His hands moved to cup her breasts as he weaved a lazy path down the side of her neck with his mouth and lips. She sucked in a breath and ground her backside into his cock, which was already hard and thick in his jeans.

She steadied herself against his thighs, stroking and learning the lines of his muscled legs. Was there a part of this man that wasn't sexy? His fingers found the buttons of her shirt, but he was too slow.

"Just yank." Her voice was almost a growl; she needed this man's hands on her breasts.

Buttons flew with one quick pull and he smoothed the shirt from her shoulders. He tugged her bra up, exposing her breasts. Her nipples puckered from the abrupt change in temperature and the anticipation. Then his hands cupped her breasts, warming and shaping and molding them. She moaned deep in her throat.

"You feel perfect in my hands. I want to taste you."

But her knees would have given out from that kind of pleasure. "I'll race you to the bed," she challenged and dove onto the ginormous king-size mattress. Stella grabbed the covers and yanked them back. "Mmm, triple sheeting. Nice."

"Only the best," he told her, his gaze tender and warm and sexy as hell.

She cupped his face. "I'll remember this forever."

He dipped his head. "Then let's continue making those memories." His lips found an über-sensitive spot beneath her ear. She sucked in his scent and this experience. She never wanted to forget this crazy night.

"What if that lady was right?" she asked. Alarm jerked though her body.

"What lady?" he asked, trailing his tongue down the column of her throat.

Moisture pooled between her thighs in response, but she couldn't force the warning away. "The lady at PharmaTest. She said we wouldn't remember tonight."

He lifted his head. A tiny line formed between his brows. Then he shook his head. "You said it yourself. Control group. We must have gotten the placebos. Everyone in that place was asleep but the four of us." Owen stared her square in the eyes and smiled. "Besides, there's no way I'm forgetting this. I mean, c'mon, you're…amazing."

And now heat pooled somewhere in the vicinity of her heart. No man had ever looked at her like Owen was at this very moment and told her she was amazing. The tension left her shoulders, and she urged him toward her. "You're right. I'd never forget you. How could I? I've never done anything even remotely like this."

"This is a first for me, too. You're a first," he said as he returned his lips to her skin, this time kissing along her collarbone.

Her lids drifted shut as a wave of sensation slid along her nerve endings. "You feel so good."

"Just wait," he whispered against the swell of her breast. "I'm going to make you feel a lot better."

He lowered his head and sighed.

But that nagging doubt wouldn't completely wane. Some cautions were just too ingrained. Had lived inside her soul for too long. Owen sighed again, but this time not from pleasure. "You're still worried," he said.

"How could you tell?"

He made a face that said *don't be ridiculous.*

"I just can't imagine how weird it would be to wake up and not remember a thing. I don't want to start all over again with you. I want to wake up and be exactly where I am right now," she told him, wiggling her hips against his. He groaned.

"I have an idea. Hotels always have notepads and paper. We'll write notes to ourselves, just in case."

"Good idea."

She scrambled off the bed in search of paper and pens, pausing only long enough to twist back into her bra and slide her shirt over her arms. Living in the moment was one thing. Doing it topless while a sexy man gazed upon you was quite another. Too unnerving. More like too distracting. She needed to keep her emotions battened down tight just a little bit longer.

A few minutes later she sat at the dinette, trying to decide what to write.

Dear Stella,

Okay, really? That was just pathetic.

In case you don't remember last night, let me just tell you that you are one lucky woman. Lucky because you get to discover all over again what a great kisser Owen is. In fact, he is everything you'd want in a man. Besides sexy as hell, he's adventurous, caring and clearly knows how to give you org—

Okay, so she didn't know that yet, but c'mon. The man gave her the quakes and shivers just by licking her nipples.

Actually, maybe this whole note-to-herself thing was kind of dumb. Sure there were strange side effects with any medication, but twenty-four-hour memory loss would be...odd. Clearly the woman had been just trying to scare them, which, frankly, was very unethical.

But could Stella really blame her? The poor lady probably would have said anything to keep them from leaving. Stella owed PharmaTest, and specifically the unknown lady, a big apology. Thankfully she didn't have to feel too guilty; drug testers used large pools of volunteers specifically because many people dropped out of studies for any number of reasons.

Across from her, Owen clicked his pen and placed it on the table. "Already done?" she asked.

He shrugged. "Didn't need to say much."

Was that a good thing?

"What did you write?" he asked, picking up the pen again and twirling it between his fingers.

She playfully held the note card to her chest. Was he nervous? Worried that she'd say something negative about him? That was kind of endearing and sweet. Of course, endearing and sweet didn't guarantee him a peek at her letter. She stuffed it in her purse.

"What I wrote is a secret. Besides, I'd only gotten a few sentences in when I realized these notes might be a waste of time anyway. In fact, just to make this interesting..."

Stella reached for a new note card and wrote in large block letters:

DON'T TRUST TONY AND HAYDEN.

His brow furrowed for a moment. Then he laughed. Man, that was one sexy laugh. The kind that made shivers tingle down her spine. "Nice one. May I?"

She handed him the pen, his rough fingers sliding along hers. Had he done that on purpose just to touch her? He'd used a perfectly good pen moments ago when he'd written his own note card.

He scribbled something on a new note card.

She turned the note so she could read it. "Oh, you have terrible handwriting. And I'm the one who's going to be a doctor." Then she read:

Don't trust anyone.

"We should make more and hide them around the room," she suggested. They spent the next few minutes writing even more notes to themselves until all the paper was used. She laughed until her shoulders shook and she had to lean against the doorframe of the bedroom.

"We are either going to find this really funny or so dumb when we wake up in the morning," he told her.

She felt the warmth of his breath and turned. When had he gotten so close? Stella gripped the hem of his polo shirt and tugged it up his chest. Owen helped her pop it over his head.

Shirtless beside her, Owen seemed so much more intimidating. His body was a finely tuned masterpiece of honed muscle. She traced the tattoo of a flame, ax and helmet on his bicep. His muscles tightened under the gentle exploration of her fingers.

"So you really are a firefighter."

"You doubted me?"

"I can see guys making up having that job and using it to their advantage. Some women find firemen kind of hot."

"The only woman I want to find it hot is you."

"How often do you carry people fireman-style?" she asked, her fingers now following the tight pec muscles of his chest. He had to be strong to battle his way through walls and burning debris to save people who were frightened and suffering from smoke inhalation.

"It's part of the training. Care for a demonstration?" he asked, his tone teasing.

"Absolutely."

"There's a price," he warned, and he began to nuzzle the back of her neck.

"And your terms are?" Whatever it was, she doubted it would be too tough a debt to pay.

"What does your note card say about me?" he asked as he licked the column of her neck.

"Mmmmm." Her knees trembled and she leaned against the tower of his body.

"Stella," he prompted.

Wow. Was he actually apprehensive about what she'd told her future self about him? She planned to keep her ideas of his orgasm-inducing abilities to herself. "It's no big deal what I wrote. We're not really going to forget tonight, and writing them was just a waste of time. What did you write about me?" she challenged. No way would he show it to her.

But Owen dug the note card from his back pocket and handed it to her.

Whatever you do, don't let Stella go without giving it a shot.

Her mouth dried. There were a lot of sexy things about Owen—the rich timbre of his voice, the muscled strength of his arms, his tight ass—but that note, his words…

that was the most erotic thing she'd discovered about him so far.

She swallowed and turned to face him. "Well, that note's not a waste of time."

"And?"

She shook her head. "Still not going to see my card."

He expression turned regretful. "And I so wanted to demonstrate my ability to hoist you over my shoulder."

He stuck by his word and didn't give in easily. She liked that about him. She liked *everything* about him.

"Do you believe in love at first sight?"

Owen's eyes widened and he swallowed. "Uh…"

Stella choked back a laugh. "Don't worry, I'm not about to profess something undying here. I'm not even sure I believe in instalove, but I do understand instalust, and man, oh, man, do I have that."

Before she could fumble out another word, she was in his arms. Enveloped in lean male muscle and woodsy cologne and an ocean of want and need. Stella met his lips, her mouth opening for a kiss so hot and amazing her entire body yielded to desire.

He hooked his arm behind her knees and then swooped her into his arms. "I thought you weren't going to carry me?" she teased, then sucked his earlobe into her mouth.

"This isn't exactly a regulation procedure," he told her.

He placed her on the soft comforter of the luxurious king-size bed and stretched out beside her. Then his mouth was on hers. Their previous kisses had been explorations, the teasing and tentative first kisses of new attraction. But now, Owen kissed her with hunger and passion and deep, deep need.

She rolled to her back and he settled between the V of her legs. She felt the hardness of his cock through her leggings and his jeans. In moments, he'd released the top buttons that hadn't flown off her shirt when she'd ordered him to rip it apart. He shoved her bra out of his way and she moaned when his hands touched skin.

"I can't wait to taste you. Taste all of you," he groaned into the side of her neck.

Stella tried to sear that sexy, guttural sound into her memory so it could never escape. But that tiny, troubling doubt poked at her again. "It would be awful to not remember this."

"We have the notes," he reminded her, and his lips lowered to her nipple, drawing it into the warmth of his mouth and making her ache.

But she could potentially wake up next to a naked man with no idea who he was or how she got there. *Disconcerting* didn't even describe that idea.

Stella squeezed her eyes shut. Ugh, all she wanted to do was enjoy this moment. To hold something so amazing and sensual in the vault of her mind so she could dust off the memory and relive it when she was deep into a shift and needed something to remind her that she was a living, breathing woman.

He circled her nipple with his tongue. This. Why couldn't she just simply enjoy this? But uncertainty still prodded her. "No, I know me. I'd yell first and ask questions later. I'd grab my clothes and race from this hotel and try never to think about it again. Or what if you wake up first and decide to get the hell out? Waking up alone with no memory might actually be worse."

"I wouldn't run," he assured her, then drew the tip of her nipple into his mouth again.

"Mmmmm." What was she protesting about? Oh, yeah. "Sure, you say that now."

He lifted his head and pinned her with his gaze. "If it makes you feel any better, I do have handcuffs in my duffel bag. We'd have to talk to each other. At least until I got them off."

"Why would that make me feel better?"

"You're worried I'll be gone in the morning. I can't leave if I'm handcuffed to you."

A rush of satisfaction made her smile. "So you want to see me in the morning? Not that I'm judging you for hooking up or anything." Could she stop herself from rambling? "I mean, clearly I've hooked up with you. It's just that I'd like to think that it's more." Nope, she couldn't stop the rambling. "Believe me, I understand. I've taken enough biology classes to understand the imperative to—"

The stubble on his cheek tickled her breasts as he skimmed up her body until they were nose to nose. His hazel eyes were dark once more. And serious. "Stella, I want to wake up in the morning with you. Order room service and have breakfast, then take you back to bed and stay here with you until we have to eat again."

"You have a way of convincing a girl. So why do you have handcuffs in your bag? Is that part of your normal, um, repertoire? Not that I'm against them or anything, but I just need to rearrange my thinking a little bit. You know…in case."

"It goes with being a firefighter. And did you just say 'in case'?"

"I'm still a little confused. Are cuffs part of the job? I don't really remember that on the tour of the fire station I took in the third grade."

He rolled off her body and began to trace light patterns on her skin with his index finger. "Sometimes couples need help getting out of their restraints, so they call 911. Firefighters usually take those emergencies."

"And this happens a lot?"

He shrugged. "Well, a lot more since that book came out. After your first restraint release, the other guys sort of gift you with a pair."

"Like a ceremony?"

"More like, uh, friendly hazing."

She held out her right hand. "Okay, cuff me."

His finger stilled. "That's the sexiest damn thing you've said. And you've said some damn sexy things."

"Ha-ha. You're getting cuffed, too, buddy."

He scooted off the bed and then lifted her until he'd flung her over his shoulder. He carried her back into the sitting room.

"I thought you weren't going to demonstrate the fireman hold until I showed you my note."

"You complaining?"

As she had a pretty good view of his ass… "Nope."

He placed her gently on her feet next to the small table where he'd dumped his duffel bag. She lowered her bra into place and refastened the top buttons.

"Why do you insist on ruining all my best work?" he asked. The metallic rip of the zipper sounded as he opened the bag, and she watched as he dug around neatly folded clothes and socks.

"Your best work?"

"I've had you nearly undressed twice now." He tugged out a box of condoms.

"Good thinking," she said as he handed them to her. Then she shrugged. "I don't know. I feel I should be clothed if I'm getting handcuffed."

"In our case, it's the exact opposite." He fumbled around until she heard the muffled sound of metal and he pulled out a pair of handcuffs. After zipping the bag closed, he placed the cuff around his wrist and clicked it in place.

"You went first."

"A show of good faith," he told her. "A gentleman always cuffs himself first. Milady?"

She lifted a brow. "That's the official etiquette in this situation?"

He nodded. "If you're uncomfortable…"

Stella took a breath and held her wrist out to him. Then pulled it back. "Wait. You're sure you have the key in there? As much as I like this firefighter tradition, I'd just as soon not be the cause of someone *else* earning his cuffs."

"Oh, the key's in there. Besides, I've learned a few tricks on how to get out of restraints."

"You know how to keep a woman intrigued." She held out arm again and he fastened the cuff around her wrist. Then she looped an arm around his neck as best she could while handcuffed to the man.

His cock hardened against her thigh.

"Show me more," she urged.

2

"YOU HAD TO wear a shirt with buttons," he said with a heavy sigh, his voice teasing.

"I'm pretty sure a firefighter can figure it out."

"I could use both hands, but then I'd have to move yours. And I like your hand right where it is."

As her hand was cupped around the hard arc of his sexy butt, Stella wasn't all that interested in moving it, either.

Had she ever been with such a gorgeous man? Most of her romantic partners had been colleagues who, like her, subsisted on food from the vending machine with few hours spent at the gym. So tonight she'd treat herself by taking her sweet time touching, tasting and savoring this amazing male specimen.

"I guess I could help you with my other hand." She lifted her left arm and clasped the material surrounding the top button. Owen's fingers brushed hers and their eyes met. Neither dropped their gaze as they freed the top button.

Mmm, mmm, mmm. This was a new experience. Men had unbuttoned her shirt before. She'd even stripped for a guy. But never had she and her partner worked together,

as a team, to take off her top. It was somehow more intimate and personal. She didn't do intimate. Or personal.

They worked their way through buttons two and three.
His knuckles brushed the newly exposed skin of her chest
and stomach. She'd make an exception for personal this
one time. Or all night.

Button number four was where the blouse-ripping had
begun, so when they reached that point, Owen slowly
slid her top off her left shoulder and then the right. He
smoothed the material down her body until it caught and
dangled on the handcuff chain between them.

His eyes crinkled in the corners and his gaze finally
left hers to focus on the problem. "I guess we didn't think
this handcuff thing all the way through. I'll go grab the
key."

But she shook her head and twined her fingers through
his. "Not yet. I like a challenge."

"Guess I should have played harder to get."

She shook her head again. "No. Just hard."

"That was kind of dirty talk, Doctor." He brushed her
lips with his. "I like it." His voice was a delicious whisper
that sent sparks of keen awareness along her nerve endings. Then Owen cupped her breast through the red silk
of her bra, and it was like he'd lit her on fire.

Stella's entire body burned and craved more. Craved
everything. Her nipple puckered against the soft material. He toyed with her, slow strokes with the pad of his
thumb, and Stella sucked in a breath.

Owen tugged on the strap of her bra. "I need to get
you out of this," he breathed into her neck. "And this
time *keep* you out."

Another blast of sexual awareness pounded her senses.
"Yes," she said, her single word long and drawn out. She
wanted to be naked. Right. Now.

"I've never picked up a man," she admitted. Not her style.

He lifted his head from her neck. A small sexy smile tugged at his lower lip. "I thought I picked *you* up."

She shook her head. "Sorry to disappoint."

His smile deepened. "Believe me, not a disappointment."

She laughed, and it made her feel good. Light. Carefree. It had been so long since she'd been wrapped in the strong arms of a gorgeous man. Not that any guy in her past equaled the sheer appeal of this man. Rugged and sexy. Capable and sensual. Owen was built like a man who knew how to work his body.

Even though she'd met him only a few hours ago, she clicked with him. Strange. She rarely formed attachments to people so quickly. Her med school training had taught her not to put a lot of stock in first impressions, but instead to form judgments based on interaction and fact. But with Owen it was all impressions and feelings and gut reactions.

"I need two hands to work the clasp of this bra and I don't want to contort your arm and hurt you."

This was no passive encounter; she was a full participant in the baring of her body to his eyes. Her every sense was heightened. All her nerve endings quickened at his touch.

She helped him out and the clasp finally, finally gave. He smoothed the material away with his palms. Stella shivered from the heat of his fingers.

His breath came out in a heavy groan. "You are beautiful, Stella."

"So are you," she told him as she traced the lean muscles of his chest. A puckered scar wrapped around his rib cage. A burn?

"We should get the key now because in another minute, I'm not going to care." Owen's hands dove into his overnight bag, stopping every few seconds to drop a quick kiss on her lips. Her nose. Her forehead.

After a few moments, he settled his hands on her shoulders and stared directly into her eyes, his gaze intent and focused and filled with desire. "Clearly I need my full concentration to find this thing," he said.

She nodded her understanding. Stella watched the play of muscles on his back as he bent down to the bag. She couldn't stop herself from stealing a caress of his bicep or leaning in to catch the woodsy outdoors scent he carried with him.

His movements became more frantic. He unzipped pockets and felt in the corners of the bag. "Those jerks."

"What?"

"Well, they left me the cuffs but not the key."

Her gaze flew to the cute black-and-white top she'd worn. Sadly, it would now be a casualty to sex. The sound of ripping fabric filled the air as she tore at the seam from hem to sleeve. Her ruined top fell silently to the carpeted floor.

"That's one way to handle it," he said, a smile lightening his face.

"The bra's going to be a problem," she warned.

"I have a pocketknife in my jeans."

"Do it." He dug in his pants until he pulled out a small, yet serviceable knife. She hissed in a breath when his fingers grazed along the sensitive skin of her shoulder. Who knew her skin was so susceptible to touch? No, *this* man's touch.

He lifted the strap and slid the blade underneath.

"Wait."

He instantly stopped. Did he think she was having second thoughts? Now?

Ha—as if she would ask him to leave her bra right where it was. "Cut in the middle of the strap. That way I can tie it in the morning."

With a few efficient moves he freed her bra from the chain between them. She tossed the bra aside and watched as it landed on the dresser in the bedroom.

"Hold out your hand, and I'll cut off the band they put on us at the testing center."

He did so and she returned the favor. Then she focused all of her attention back on the sexy hot man in front of her.

Owen pulled her into his arms. "I believe you were licking my ear and talking dirty."

"Pretty talented, aren't I? I can lick and talk at the same time," she teased. He was about to reply, but she silenced him when she traced her tongue along his ear and sucked the lobe into her mouth. "Does this give you any ideas?" she asked after a moment.

He nodded. "Too many good ones." His free hand caressed and stroked her breast, then moved lower. Butterflies flapped to attention inside her stomach as his fingers rubbed the bare skin above her leggings. He dipped his hand between her legs, stroking and teasing her through her underwear until her legs grew weak.

"Owen, you have to slow down," she moaned into his neck.

Stroke.

Her clit grew heavy and tingly. "This feels too good."

"Nothing can feel too good," he told her, nibbling at the tender skin above her collarbone.

Stroke.

Her inner muscles began to clamp deliciously.

"Owen, I'm going to come too soon."

Strooookkkke.

"Then you can come again," he said, his voice tight.

But Stella also had a free hand, and she could play the tormenting game, too. She trailed her fingers down the hard ridge of muscle lining his spine, then smoothed her palms along the ridged rows of muscle on his stomach until she found the waistband of his jeans. His cock was a long ridge beneath the zipper and she quickly freed him. He sprang into her hand. Smooth and hard. She circled the head of his cock with her thumb. She'd meant only to torment him the way he was tormenting her, but feeling the evidence of his desire for her made Stella want him to plunge inside her. Fill her. Thrust until they both came.

"I don't want to wait, Owen."

"Yeah. No, I—"

She cut off his words by dragging him to the large bay window in the bedroom. Below, a large, beautiful courtyard with lights in the trees and a meandering path through flowers beckoned lovers for a late-night stroll. But not these lovers. No, Stella wanted only to be alone with this man in the bedroom of this amazing suite.

With a press of her finger, a filmy curtain drifted down. The street lights faded but the glow of the Dallas skyline still filtered through. Stella dropped to the curved bench beneath the window, the diamond-tufted cushion soft beneath her back.

"Here," she urged. "Make love to me here."

Owen's eyes flared, but she couldn't read his expression in the now darkened room.

He reached for the band of her leggings at her waist. He groaned as he slid her pants down her legs. "Those are the sexiest damn panties I've ever seen."

She was kind of partial to the black scalloped lace herself. Stella wore nothing but scrubs all day, every day, so she needed the feel of silk and lace on her skin. Actually, right now she needed the feel of this man's hands back on her skin. She lifted her hips to help him draw her panties down.

"Just like that," he said, and his finger brushed along the curls between her legs.

"Hmm?"

"When I'm inside you, I want you to meet me just like this."

Could she come because of a man's words? But the thought fled from her mind quickly, replaced by the all-consuming images of his hard length deep inside her, stroking her as she raised her hips to meet his every thrust.

Owen reached for one of the wrapped condoms.

"Here, let me." She tore the top of the package off, then grasped his cock, caressing him softly. She watched his face in the dim light as she touched him. His eyes were closed, his jaw tight with need. He stroked her with the barest of touches as she slid the condom in place. Slowly.

"Now that's how to put on a condom," he told her with a half groan.

Stella laughed, feeling carefree and sexy and so, so needy.

His free hand clasped her chin. He caressed her cheek with his thumb.

"You ready?" he asked.

So ready.

Stella nodded and he stepped between her legs, grabbed her by the hips and pulled her ass to the end of the cushioned bench seat. He teased her clit with the pad his thumb. "You're so wet."

She shivered at his touch, and then he slipped his finger inside her at an agonizingly slow pace. Stella sucked in a breath as delicious tingles bombarded her body. But as desperate as she was to have him buried deep inside her so she could lose herself in the powerful wave of sex, it had been a long time for her. She hadn't had a boyfriend since she'd started med school, and…wow, had it really been over two years? She began to count in her—

The head of his penis replaced his gently exploring finger, and all thoughts of math and time and calendars fled. Now she was all about sensation.

With a shift of his hips, Owen slid inside her with a slow and steady thrust. Her inner muscles instantly clamped along his length and she held her breath.

"You with me, Stella?" he asked, his deep voice strained. "You're so tight. You feel amazing."

She lifted her eyes to his face, and while it was too dark to read his expression, Stella felt the tension emanating from his body. Oh, she was with him. Stella nodded.

But still he didn't move. Sweat broke out along his brow, proof of his effort to hold back so he wouldn't hurt her.

"I'm with you, Owen. I want you so bad."

Slowly, as if the man didn't trust himself, he withdrew from her only slightly, then thrust inside again. She moaned as a surge of pleasure made her shiver. "More. Again."

Owen didn't hesitate this time, pulling from her body and thrusting over and over. He easily found the tempo that drew the deepest moans and most powerful trembles from her body.

She'd been right. Owen knew exactly how to work his body. And hers. Stella locked her feet behind his back and his free hand found her breast. He rubbed the tip with his thumb and she lifted her hips to meet his thrusts.

She grabbed the hand that was cuffed to hers and he twined his fingers through hers. An unexpected wave of tender intimacy rushed through her and sensation exploded inside her. Her muscles clenched with the power of her orgasm, and her shoulders and hands shook.

His big, beautiful body pumped into her, and then he came, too, his moan lingering in the air like something to be savored. He slumped beside her on the narrow bay window bench, their cuffed hands still intertwined. Her breathing was harsh but his was even more ragged.

She smiled, content to watch the shadowed lights of the city through the sheerness of the curtain.

After a moment he propped himself up on his elbow and looked down into her face. He ran his finger along the curve of her jaw.

"I want to make some joke right now about how I still have a fire that you need to put out."

"I think I could help you out with that. Or I could tease you about how you're almost a doctor so you should have the perfect prescription for this discomfort I get right here." He drew her hand to his cock. "It happens whenever I'm around you, Doc."

She gave him a mock stern look. "Sounds serious."

"But we'd never make those kinds of jokes."

"Nah, nothing that corny," she agreed. Then Owen swooped down and landed his mouth against hers and kissed her. As he cupped her face, his tongue slid between her lips. Her free hand went to the back of his neck to draw him closer. Stella pressed herself against his chest, giving as much to their kiss as she took.

And suddenly they were no longer playful, or looking to make corny jokes, and she was not chalking their night up to ending her man-fast.

"I want to spend the weekend with you," he said.

Had there been sweeter words? His statement was exactly what she wanted to hear, and she hadn't even realized she'd wanted it.

"Me, too."

"Just not on this uncomfortable bench. I barely fit." And then he swooped her up in his arms and dumped her on the bed. He stretched out beside her and she rested her head on his chest. His heart pumped a steady rhythm beneath her head, enticing her to doze. "Now that's more like it," he said, his voice heavy with sleep.

She stifled a yawn behind her hand. "I think our eventful night is catching up with me."

"Same."

"I mean, I've never been kicked out of a roller rink before."

Owen's chest rose as he chuckled. "I'll never get a big head around you."

She lifted her head to gaze at the glowing red numbers on the bedside clock. "It's been hours since PharmaTest gave us that medication. Even if we weren't on the placebo, with the passage of time and the adrenaline we've burned through since escaping that place, I'm thinking any immediate effects would have passed. Guess we really didn't need the cuffs. Memories of tonight still intact." *Forever.*

"I'd search again for the keys, but I have this gorgeous brunette pinning me to the bed."

She snuggled against his side. "You complaining?"

"No, ma'am."

"You know, I kind of feel sorry for that lady who checked us out."

"Larissa?" he asked.

Stella snapped her fingers. "That's her name—good

memory. Poor woman. There she was, just trying to do her job, and she wound up with the four of us."

"And she was right. Participating in medical studies like that is important to me, and we made it way more difficult for her."

Stella bit back the urge to ask him more about why he'd participated in the drug trial. She'd been volunteering for medical experiments since her freshman year of college. Growing up in a house of physicians, she understood the value of medical research. But Owen had suggested he'd lost someone. This drug trial must have been much more personal for him.

"How'd you end up at PharmaTest? The plates on your truck say Colorado."

"The building used to be the volunteer center for a different organization. Thought I might kill a few hours there until I met up with my family. Which reminds me, I should call my mom so she's not waiting."

"We should also call Larissa. Just to let her know we're okay."

"Good idea. I think the number was on the ID bracelets."

Stella slid out of bed and started for the dresser across the room, only to be jerked back. She lost her balance and landed on the bed with a flop. "That didn't go as planned."

He leaned over her, his head upside down in relation to hers, and kissed her forehead. "Guess we'll have to go together."

He walked behind her toward her partially torn blouse. It had been so cute at one point. Oh, well, no use mourning when her top had given its life for her pursuit of pleasure.

"Please tell me you aren't going to try to put it on for a third time."

"Hadn't crossed my mind." Yet. She tugged her phone from the pocket of her discarded shirt and grabbed the PharmaTest bands off the dresser, Owen close behind. She turned and his gaze lifted.

"Were you checking out my butt?"

"Not anymore."

Because now his gaze flipped between her breasts and her eyes. Her nipples hardened like they'd been caressed, and Stella smiled. She enjoyed being desired by this man. She wanted nothing more than to slip between the sheets beside him again.

After carefully dialing the number on the bands, she pressed the speaker function on her phone. The call went to voice mail.

"Hi, this message is for Larissa at PharmaTest. This is Stella Holbrook."

"And Owen Perkins," he said into the phone.

"We just called to let you know we're great and you have nothing to worry about. In fact, we're staying in the most beautiful room on the second floor at the Market Gardens. We hope we didn't cause too many problems for you when we bailed on the test earlier. Bye."

Stella pushed End.

"Do you feel better?"

"Yes, and we made that call just in time. My phone died." Stella left her phone on the bedside table and tossed the wristbands into the trash. After the shortest conversation a man could have with his family, Owen closed his phone and leaned against the stack of fluffy pillows. Then she settled against his chest and closed her eyes.

He drew a lazy pattern on her back. "Stella, this was

kind of a rough day for me, and tonight, being with you… just, thanks."

"Mmm."

"You falling asleep on me?"

"Who are you again?" she asked, her voice heavy with sleep.

Beside her, Owen tensed. "Are you serious?" he asked.

"Just kidding," Stella told him, her mouth wide with a smile. But she couldn't keep her eyes from closing again.

His arm tightened around her shoulders while his cuffed hand gently squeezed hers. "Say my name," he urged.

"Owen." Then, like a patient inescapably lulled by the pull of anesthesia, she succumbed to sleep.

STELLA'S EYELIDS FLUTTERED open slowly. It was a rare day when she woke up without the help of an alarm. On one side, she was deliciously warm. But on the other, her backside was frozen against the hard, cold marble of a…bathtub?

She forced her eyes open. She wasn't snuggled into a cozy blanket; her head was cradled on…on a warm male thigh.

And the man…whoever he was…his body clearly liked what it assumed would be happening next.

"Ahh!" Her voice was a cross between a yelp and a shriek. Stella scrambled away from the man, her hand slapping against his skin. She flew up and off the stranger at a record-setting pace, only for something to catch her wrist and force her back down. Hard.

Her eyes met his, then lowered. Was that a flame tattoo on his…

"Who the hell are you?" she asked, looking up. Way up.

His eyes narrowed, the brown in his hazel eyes growing dark. "Who am I? Who are you? And careful, you almost got me. You've got a mean left arm."

Yeah, because her right arm was cuffed to his left. "Sorry, I was startled. I don't wake up every morning with a man's hardware staring me in the face."

"This is new to me, too," he mumbled. "This marble is cold. How about we get out of the tub?"

And maybe they could find him a robe or something, because…wow. When she wasn't noticing his tattoo or his hardware, she realized this man packed a pretty serious punch. A solid chest with that perfect T of chest hair. Ripped and toned, the guy worked out. Religiously. Normally she didn't go for the big-and-strong type. She preferred the science geeks, like her.

She wrapped her hand around the corner of the black-and-white marble tub, and together they stood. She sucked in a breath.

"You okay?" he asked.

"Just a little stiff."

He rotated his shoulders. "Yeah, the tub was cramped."

But the bathroom was bigger than the kitchen in her apartment. Although the soaker tub dominated the space, a two-person rainfall shower shouted *come rub shower gel all over your lover*. And whose design idea was it to put floor-to-ceiling mirrors on every wall? Everywhere she looked, she was blasted by images of his naked body. And hers. But mostly his. Seriously, his ass was like something out of a plastic surgeon's wish-list book.

She stepped out of the tub and onto the fuzzy bathmat, and the man beside her followed. They padded into a bedroom. A king-size bed with all the sheets and blankets askew greeted them. Of course. Decorative pillows looked to have been launched all over the room and an economy-size box of condoms lay on the nightstand.

"At least we practiced safe sex."

"Always," he assured her.

A bubble of panic rose and lodged somewhere in her chest. Stella took a deep breath. *You are not going to panic. There's a logical explanation.* Then Stella realized she wasn't panicking. Which was odd. Why wasn't she freaking out?

Work the problem.

She'd start with the man beside her. Just because they were alone in a hotel room with a box of condoms didn't mean they'd actually had sex. One-night stands had never been her thing, and despite nothing but studying, tests and observation for the past two plus years, she doubted she'd turned over the casual-sex leaf simply because she finally had a well-deserved break in her schedule.

Stella faced him then. She must have appeared more worried than she felt, because his hazel eyes softened. Gorgeous eyes. Gorgeous body. Yeah, she'd probably straddled this guy half a dozen times last night. Plus, her body felt deliciously exercised.

He seemed embarrassed, which was a big point in his favor.

"I don't usually forget a woman's name."

Just when she'd thought this scenario couldn't get more awkward.

"Stella," she supplied. She raised her arm. "And the handcuffs?"

He shook his head. "Not my thing, but if a lady requests it…" He shrugged as if to say, *Who am I to say no?*

"You think these are mine?" Ugh, her voice teetered on sounding like a shriek.

The interest fled from his eyes, replaced with concern. "How much of last night do you remember?"

3

LARISSA WINSTON HAD been able to keep it together until she checked out her last patient. Then she locked the office door, turned the placard to Closed and leaned her forehead against the wall. *In through your mouth, out through your nose.*

Thirty seconds. She'd allow herself only thirty seconds to freak out completely, and then she'd start working on a plan. Her hands shook and she squeezed her eyes shut, stifling the shriek that had been building inside her since she'd begun checking out, so slowly, this morning's test subjects.

Twenty-five seconds. So she'd lost four patients. *Four.*

Twenty seconds. The shaking became a full-on assault on her stomach. Larissa swallowed several times to keep from throwing up, and the wave of nausea passed.

Fifteen seconds. She kicked off her shoes and wiggled her toes. The muscles in her feet and calves relaxed. The pent-up tension and stress eased just a bit and she began to unwind.

Ten seconds. She finished out her freak-out with a mantra. *Don't rush. Don't panic. Don't make it worse than it already is.*

Time's up. Larissa wiped the sweat from the back of her neck and secured her red hair with the elastic she'd slipped on her wrist. She opened her eyes and slid her shoes back on her feet. Freak-out done. Slowly she switched off the lights in the reception area and turned the wand on the miniblinds. All normal. All tasks she'd performed dozens of times.

She slumped on the couch in the staff lounge. Now that she'd gotten the inevitable losing-it portion of the morning out of the way, she could find the bright side. Because there was always a bright side.

The four runaways had signed the waivers. *Ding ding ding.* Yes! First bright side, and it was a biggie. She'd warned the test subjects of the dangers of leaving and tried to keep them in place, and they'd left against her advice.

What the hell had happened last night? No one had ever reacted so strangely, and then *boom*—there'd been four. In the past, Larissa usually spent Thursday night of the test herding sleepy patients to their private bunks or offering board games and drinks to them in the patient activity room. Her Friday mornings were then passed gently waking patients, pushing caffeine-rich coffee onto the volunteers and completing paperwork.

But those four hadn't been lethargic or anywhere near sleepy. They'd been charged. Racing into the night. Hooking up!

They'd released her of liability, she *could* let it go. Volunteer subjects fell out of research studies all the time. She could just mark these four down in that column—no-shows and dropouts. It was just that—and this was what negated that booming big bright side she'd discovered earlier— no one had ever bailed while under the influence of the medication. Funding was tightly competitive, and grants weren't given to drug trials with blank spaces. Dr. Durant's work depended on that money. She needed to follow up on the runaways. Who knew what those four had done last night? Could she be so lucky that they'd all just gone home to sleep it off?

Investigating what happened to the four wasn't part of her job, but it was the right thing to do. And not just for the individual test subjects, but also because of the potential of HB121. If it worked the way Dr. Durant claimed it did, the drug would save countless lives. And if it was corny to say she wanted to leave the world a little better than how she found it, then slap on the butter.

The phone rang, and her stomach flip-flopped when the caller ID revealed Dr. Durant's number. Panic replaced the flips. He never called. His MO was to drop by the offices, looking scholarly and sexy, to pick up the results himself. Had he found out somehow about the lost patients?

Her fingers shook as she picked up the receiver. "PharmaTest. This is Larissa Winston."

"Ms. Winston, this is Mitch, er...Dr. Durant."

Her fingers squeezed around the handle. "Good morning, Dr. Durant." Had he just referred to himself as Mitch to her?

"I'll be around the PT offices earlier than usual. I thought if you hadn't eaten we could catch some breakfast. Together."

Panic upon panic layered with more panic twisted up inside her. He'd arrive before she could track down the four missing patients, and she'd have to confess that she'd lost them. "Oh, that's okay. You don't have to do that."

"I want to. You're an important part of the HB121 team, Larissa. Of my team."

She squeezed her eyes tightly shut. He'd just called her Larissa. He'd never done that before. And had there been a special emphasis on the word *my*? Did Dr. Durant think of her as more than just the tech who took care of the test subjects? Larissa's roommate, Kay, said that when Larissa wasn't looking, the man could barely tear his gaze away from her. She'd just laughed it off and chalked it up to Kay's attempt to instill a little false courage in Larissa so she'd make the first move toward the über-hot doc.

Her shaky fingers found the hem of her scrubs and she began bending over the material in tight fold after fold. "I, uh…really have a lot to do here."

"Oh."

An uneasy quiet hung between them over the line. Dr. Durant actually sounded disappointed. Like his invitation hadn't been that of a coworker politely asking another to tag along for a meal. Was it the goddess of irony or the god of bad luck she had to thank for messing up this opportunity? Any other day, she would have been offering to pick him up after even the slightest encouragement.

"I guess I'll see you when I stop by to look over the results. Bye, Ms. Winston," he said, the politely professional Dr. Mitch Durant back in place.

After dropping the phone into the cradle, Larissa hugged her legs to her chest and rested her forehead on her knees. No, no, no. Why now?

She had to fix this mess. Larissa owed it to Dr. Mitch Durant. Then she'd ask *him* to breakfast. And lunch and dinner or brunch or second breakfast or whatever the man would agree to.

Something had to be wrong with Dr. Durant's formula for those four volunteers to react so differently from the previous subjects. Dr. D tweaked the ingredients from time to time. If he'd fine-tuned something the wrong way, she had to tell him. He'd also want to interview the four missing subjects. Then she'd have to tell him she'd lost them. Larissa had let the man down. She rubbed her neck and squeezed her eyes shut. She hated that the most.

The phone rang, and a jolt of excitement energized her despite her all-nighter at PharmaTest. But the caller ID revealed it was only her roommate, Kay.

"You wearing the tight pencil skirt?"

She was in comfy salmon PharmaTech scrubs. "Yes," Larissa replied. She could always change later. After turning the man down, she didn't plan to greet Mitch wearing sloppy scrubs.

"And the do-me heels I loaned you? I'm telling you, those have never failed. What time is Doctor Hottie supposed to get there?"

"I asked you to stop calling him that. I'm not even sure he'll show."

Her roommate's knowing laugh was clear through the phone line. "Oh, he'll show. I mean, honestly, I've never seen two people more in lust than you and the doc. You'd think nature, in the interest of propagating the species, would have given one of you some idea of how to express sexual interest to the other, but no. You'd be hopeless without me."

Any other morning, Larissa would have eaten up her roommate's words with a spoon. But this morning, the man she'd thought was only interested in his research had asked her out for breakfast, and she'd had to turn him down flat.

After the higher-ups at PharmaTest learned of last night's fiasco, she'd be fired. This morning would probably be the last time she'd ever catch a glimpse of the sexy doc who'd starred in all her fantasies for the past three years. *If* he showed up. Her heartbeat kicked up at just the thought of seeing him. She was pathetic.

The little red light flashed on the side of the phone,

indicating a voice mail. She'd checked the PharmaTest voice mail sometime after midnight and there'd been no messages. Her breath caught. All four patients had left wearing their PharmaTest badges last night. Had they discovered the tags around their wrists and called?

"...just take off those sexy glasses of his, grab him by the tie and demand a little downward-facing doctor."

"Kay, I have to go." Larissa disconnected the call without waiting for a response. Then she pressed the voice mail button.

"Hi, this message is for Larissa at PharmaTest. This is Stella Holbrook."

Larissa sucked in a breath. Test subject ninety-two. *Yes!*

"And Owen Perkins." Still with the handsome fire-fighter. And those two had definitely left with Thirty-Five and Seventy-Eight. Stella straightened her spine. Could she be so lucky that they were all still together?

"We just called to let you know we're great and you have nothing to worry about. In fact, we're staying in the most beautiful room on the second floor at the Market Gardens. We hope we didn't cause too many problems when we bailed on the test earlier. Bye."

Larisa shot up from her chair with such force the thing rolled away and bounced against the wall. The Market Gardens wasn't too far. After changing out of her scrubs, Larissa raced to where she'd left her shoes, grabbed her purse and keys and was out the door.

STELLA TRIED TO THINK. Did she remember last night? No. In fact, she couldn't recall a single detail from Thursday at all. "The last thing I remember was Wednesday after-noon," she told this tall, sexy stranger beside her, hating the way that sounded.

A line formed between his brows, and he rubbed the back of his neck. "Wednesday. That's the last day I remember, too. I'd loaded up the truck to drive to Dallas."

"You're not from around here?" she asked, her voice rising despite the fact that she had warned herself not to freak out. Stella couldn't decide whether her sexy hookup not being from the metroplex was a point in his favor or not.

"Colorado." His hazel eyes were a bit unfocused, like his mind was busy trying to put together the events of the past twenty-four hours instead of staying with their conversation. "Actually, I do remember hitting the road, but not arriving in Dallas. We are in Dallas, right?"

"As far as I know." She angled her head toward the window. "Only one way to find out." Stella tried to push back the gauzy curtain, but it was on some sort of automatic system. She pressed the button located on the wall with force. The curtain rose and the Dallas skyline stretched before them. She breathed out a sigh of relief. "Looks like you made it."

"Why were we in the tub?"

She shrugged. "We're in Texas. I'm guessing tornado."

"This time of year?"

A lot of people not from the plains states assumed where there was rain, a funnel cloud was sure to follow, regardless of the season. But this guy knew fall wasn't usually tornado season. So that was something she could add to her inventory and assessment. *Knows the area.*

"If you have a better explanation, let's hear it," she told him.

"I'm guessing we were fulfilling that bubble-bath fantasy you've wanted to try out. Great choice. I'm the man for the job."

Her lips pressed together in a tight line but she focused

her gaze on Reunion Tower. Tonight The Orb would light up bright and beautiful. It was one of her favorite things about Dallas.

"I don't think so," she managed, trying to figure out her next steps. *Get dressed and get out.* Wonderful, she had a plan.

"Not a morning person?" he asked. "Good to know."

Stella whirled away from the window. "You won't need to know that because you won't be seeing me again."

His eyes widened for a moment, and he coughed. Then his gaze lifted first to her eyes, then her mouth, and finally settled somewhere behind her shoulder. He seemed to be doing everything he could not to check out her breasts. Nice touch, not ogling the naked woman in front of him. Made him a little more likeable. Especially after that morning-person crack. She was perfectly delightful in the morning.

She started to say something, but her eyes landed on his pecs.

The human form was anything but remarkable to her. Until a few moments ago, she'd thought nudity was now a nonissue to her. Stella had seen the human body brand-new and screaming in the delivery room and generously gifted after death in her gross-anatomy class. To her, the body had become nothing more than parts to assess and categorize.

Unless those parts were ripped abs, strong hold-me-all-night arms and accentuated by a flame tattoo…

Okay, stop. Stop right there. Sure, her man-drought was over, and even though she couldn't remember all the fun she'd (surely) had exploring this man's angles and planes, it was a new day now, and playtime was over.

She shook her head. *Good one, Stella. Sure, nudity means nothing to you. Ha!* Life had a funny way of throwing all the assumptions you made about yourself completely off-kilter. Maybe she should follow his lead. Eyes up and away from bulging biceps and sculpted pecs.

Get dressed and get out.

Oh, yes, her plan.

"I'm not actually opposed to seeing you again," he said. There was a slight drawl in his voice that indicated he'd spent a long time in Texas.

She shifted her weight from one leg to the other.

"So, um, you...?" she began, focusing her eyes on the wall behind him.

Now why was his answering chuckle the kind that made her bare toes curl against the plush carpet?

"I'm a firefighter, stationed along the Sawatch Range in Colorado."

Stella pictured the tall peaks of the Rockies dotted with gorgeous pines. But she also pictured the kind of man who thrived on adrenaline spikes and the rush of adventure. The kind of man who kept the ER hopping with broken bones, lacerations and abrasions. Stella didn't date emergency room frequent flyers. Strange that she'd hooked up with him last night.

"I'm in medical school, almost done." She tried sitting down on the bed, only to be confronted with the muscled breadth of his shoulders and a line of hair that shadowed his chest and lowered in a tempting line toward—

She stood up quickly. "So, are you returning to Dallas or just a visit?" *Please say visit. Please say visit.*

"Family thing."

Her shoulders sagged. Good. Once out of these handcuffs, she'd never have to see him again. Then her stomach lurched. Really? The possibility of not seeing him was what got a reaction from her body?

Again, shouldn't she be more alarmed?

"Are you worried about this?" she asked, focusing on her toes.

"Worried about what—the hot woman? The handcuffs? Or the fact that I can't remember a damn thing?"

"All of it," she answered with a shrug. Then she bit the inside of her cheek as she waited for his answer. And no, she would not let her breath go all shallow because he'd called her hot.

"I feel like I should be worried. I always play it safe with sex."

"That explains the huge box of condoms," she said, aiming for a little levity.

"It's more than safe sex. I want to *know* the woman I'm with."

And then her breath did get all shallow, and her pulse became thready. The way he said *know*, as if he'd recognize the touch of a particular woman's skin with his eyes closed. As if he basked in his lover's pleasured moans, memorized her taste, delighted in heating her blood. Excitement thrummed through her. Her nipples hardened and— No!

She'd adopted that man-fast for a reason—she was about to go through the most grueling stretch of her training so far. How she did in the next year would not only allow her to graduate at the top of her class but also open doors to the best hospitals around the country.

She forced her gaze to focus on anything but this beautiful man in front of her and what he made her want.

And that's when she spotted a rumpled swath of black fabric lying in a discarded lump on the carpet. With an excited cry, she began to race toward what had to be her leggings.

She'd taken only three steps when her arm caught on

the cuffs and she was yanked back. How did people even begin to think handcuffs were sexy?

The big, seductive stranger steadied her against the heated warmth of his chest. Her fingers clutched sinewy muscles and smooth heated skin. Oh, that's why people thought handcuffs were sexy.

"Going somewhere?" he asked, and Stella discovered a delightful hint of teasing green in the hazel of his eyes.

"Clearly not without help," she grumbled, but she honestly couldn't make it sound too cranky. See—she was perfectly delightful in the morning.

She cleared her throat. "Sir, would you care to accompany me into the drawing room? I believe I may have spotted last night's attire." Yep, she'd brought out the big guns—formal manners. Because really, how else were you supposed to conduct yourself when you were handcuffed to a sexy man, naked, with no memory of said man or how you got completely in the buff?

He nodded, and the two of them crossed to the black fabric. Black leggings. Ugh, she didn't even remember putting them on the night before. Which nicely bookended with not remembering taking them off. Although somehow she suspected the man beside her had taken them off for her. A quiver of delight settled between her legs as she imagined his fingers on her bare skin.

Get dressed and get out.

Yes, but were his palms calloused or smooth? Had his hands shaken with pent-up desire or had he caressed her skin with the sure strokes of a man who knew exactly how to touch a woman to make her need him more?

No. Don't go there. Tamp that down right now. There would not be an idealized replay of a night she couldn't even remember.

Her panties were not in sight, but with her handcuff

buddy's help, she stepped into her leggings anyway. In the brighter light of the living area, her skin appeared flushed. The faint coloration of a tiny love bruise was forming on her inner thigh, and her muscles ached with a kind of sensuous lethargy—all due to the man she couldn't escape. She gripped the waistband of her leggings in an effort to jerk herself clothed. The slide of the knit fabric up her legs was like a taunting caress, and the handcuffs meant she was truly stuck.

"Good. I'll think better," he mumbled.

Did he mean...? Was he actually...? Did her nudity disturb him? Stella wasn't used to big sensual men like this one finding her attractive. Or if they had, she'd been too tired or too busy to notice. A shiver sizzled down her back and her breathing hitched. And suddenly she was all too aware of his naked skin. And hers. Ugh, a flush spread across her chest and her nipples hardened.

Yeah, she had to get dressed and get out.

But what about him? Get him clothed or get him uncuffed? Okay, that was a no-win situation. She needed both to happen. Now. She scanned the room for the rest of their clothes.

A note card caught her attention in the corner.

"Do you see that?" she asked, pointing at a paper on the intimate dinette for two. A delicate scalloped tablecloth decorated the table along with fresh Texas wildflowers and lilies, heart-shaped chocolates and candles. The romantic mood in this setting would strangle a valentine.

They rushed to the wooden dinette, the sweet scent of daylilies filling her nose. Large block letters spelled READ ME on the card propped against the vase, where they were sure to spot it.

"That's my handwriting," he told her. He lifted the

note from the table and unfolded the paper. "'You're in danger,'" he read.

A twinge of alarm settled between her shoulder blades. "You wouldn't—" she began.

"What?"

Stella pointed to the mantel above the fireplace. "There's another note. My handwriting this time."

Any other day she'd take a moment to appreciate the masterpiece of the art deco fireplace with its beveled edges and rounded corners. Black-and-white ceramic tile surrounded the firebox, finished off with a highly polished wooden mantel carved with the geometric designs popular at the time. Of course she would have left a note for herself here.

She unfolded the paper. "'Only trust Owen.'"

The man beside her sucked in a breath.

"I'm guessing you're Owen."

He nodded. "Owen Perkins."

She crumpled the note in her palm. Danger? Trust? What had they gotten themselves into last night? "It's like we woke up in one of those urban-legend stories."

"At least we didn't leave a note for ourselves to call 911."

"Yet. Look, we left ourselves more notes." Now that they'd spotted the first two, their eyes were opened to the others strewn about the room.

Owen went to the right.

Stella went to the left. The chain between them forced them back together. His hands curved around her shoulders as he steadied her. The man was built like an immovable boulder.

"Easy," he said, his breath ruffling the hair at her temple. The man might be as solid as a rock formation, but his voice was soothing. Reassuring. It was also sexy as hell. Mountainous men weren't usually her style, but she could see the appeal. In a one-time deal.

"We've got to get out of these cuffs. Where's the key?"

His brow lifted. "What makes you think that they're mine?" His gaze dropped to the chain between them. "Actually, these could belong to me. Sort of."

"Yeah. Uh-huh. Thought so. So, grab the key."

"Probably in my bag." He scanned the room. "There it is." His voice was warm and soothing, with just a hint of nonaggressive authority. It instantly put her at ease.

Wow. That was some bedside manner he'd cultivated. Her bedside manner sucked.

Relief that they'd soon be free lifted her spirits. "Key first. Then the notes." She could almost smile.

And then he grabbed her hand and twined her fingers between his before crossing the soft carpet toward the bag.

Stella wasn't a hand holder. She'd left that behind with high school dances and Friday night football games. But this, the intimacy of her hand in his, was kind of nice. Right up there with his reassuring voice that said they would figure out this whole weird morning together.

Only trust Owen.

What happened to *get dressed and get out*?

His bag was more like a duffel, something used for an overnight or quick weekend trip. Maybe that's why she'd chosen him last night to end the man-fast—because she'd never have to see him again. But then why the handcuffs?

Stella examined her skin under the metal. No chafing ran around her wrist. You'd better believe there'd be a ton of abrasions if that handcuff had been placed on her by force.

A balled-up pair of socks lay forgotten on the floor near his duffel. A T-shirt teetered half in and half out of the bag. Like they'd already ransacked his belongings. Had they previously searched the bag for the key and failed to find it? Her heartbeat revved up, but she tamped down the panic. No need to assume the worst.

Owen dove his hands inside, taking out more folded clothes until the bag was empty. Then he began sliding his fingers along the inside and searching through the zippered pockets.

"Nothing," he finally told her.

"Did you find any toothpaste?"

He tossed her one of those tiny travel-size tubes, and she twisted off the top and squeezed some onto her finger without jerking his hand around too much. He stretched out his finger, and she squeezed some on for him, too. Then they both finger-brushed their teeth.

"Maybe in your pants pocket?" she suggested once that task was complete.

His jeans lay carelessly tossed on the back of the couch. Clearly they'd been in a hurry last night. In a hurry to get naked.

Together they crossed to the couch, and Owen lifted off his pants. Now, he could have been in a bigger hurry to put those jeans back on, as far as she was concerned. He'd been on the right track earlier; *she* could think better with those pants on him. Change fell out of his pocket as well as his car keys, but no handcuff key.

Beside her, Owen donned his jeans, and she raised and lowered her arm as he slid the jeans in place. The backs of her knuckles grazed the hair-roughened stretch of his thigh as he slid the denim up his legs. Her mouth dried. How many times had she stroked those muscled thighs last night? Straddled his hips? When you were with a man built like a statue to honor the gods, you caressed and tongued and—

"You gotta give me a break." His voice was ragged and raw.

Stella met his gaze. "What?"

"C'mon. You're looking at me like you want to touch me."

Hell, she wanted to do a lot more than touch. Her gaze lowered to his chest. Solid and dusted with hair. Perfect. An image of her working down the fly of his jeans flashed through her mind and all her senses reacted.

A memory? No, more like wishful thinking in the present. Because working down the fly is what she would have done last night. And after she'd slid the zipper down, she would have shoved the soft material off his hips just far enough to free his cock. She'd have licked his collarbone. Nipped his skin with her teeth. Trailed her tongue down his body until she reached his—

"Like that. Don't do that," he hissed between his teeth. "I'm doing everything I can to…"

"To what?"

"To not lift you onto my shoulder, carry you into that bedroom, drop you on that mattress and make up for what I don't remember."

"Owen, I—"

He squeezed his eyes shut. "Don't say my name. You say it like a moan. Don't look at me like you want my hands all over your body." He gripped her shoulders and his gaze locked with hers.

There was hunger there. Hunger for her.

"I want you, Stella. But not like this. So I'm about to suggest something I've never thought I'd suggest—let's find your bra."

Perspiration beaded on her forehead. Damn, she needed both of them to be fully covered. Head to toe. In one of those long flannel granny robes. Something completely unsexy—a housecoat.

She spotted the dark silk of her bra on the dresser in the bedroom, a pocketknife beside it. Stella quickly reached for the lacy wisp of fabric.

Owen turned his back to her as best he could. Which was kind of sweet since she'd been beside him completely naked since they woke up together. She stifled a groan when she spotted the marks on his shoulder.

"You okay?" he asked.

She'd scratched him. The signs of her nails were crisscrossed along his back. Stella had never marked a lover before. Sex in the past had been mutual pleasure. A release of natural bodily desires. Nothing so carnal or primal.

Last night must have been something.

"Stella?"

"It's just that I…appear to have…scratched you." Facing up to her own primitive behavior last night was a little shocking. She'd allowed emotion and cravings to take over her judgment—and she'd apparently enjoyed the hell out of it. The feeling was foreign and uncomfortable and just a tiny bit intriguing. She gently touched one of the red welts. "That doesn't hurt too bad, does it?"

He flinched at her touch, and her hand dropped away. "I'll live."

She slipped the bra strap over her left shoulder, but the right strap dangled in two pieces. The pocketknife explained that.

"Well, we weren't naked when we were handcuffed. My bra strap is a major casualty from last night. I'll need you to tie it."

Owen turned, but she rotated away before she could spot his eyes. She just didn't need that distraction at the moment.

He tied the ends together and she was finally covered. Mostly. Her shirt was around here somewhere. Stella began to scan the room, but something else caught her eye. "There's a note in here, too. My bra must have been covering it."

He lifted the paper from the dresser and unfolded the next note. "'Don't trust Larissa Winston.' Does the name mean anything to you?"

She shook her head.

"Me, neither. Let's grab the rest of these notes and see what we can figure out. We can line them all up on the table and try to piece them together like a puzzle."

"Good idea. There don't appear to be any more in the bedroom," she said.

They returned to sitting area, but this time Owen didn't reach for her hand. She ignore the fact that she even noticed.

Another note waited on the TV, and another near a discreetly tucked away minifridge. They found their shirts near two overturned wine glasses lying near a curved bench by the large bay window. She slid into her shirt while he tugged a polo over his head.

"You had the easy one," she told him.

He lifted a brow. "Oh?"

"I have buttons. Or, at least, three of them."

Sometime last night, he or she or both of them had grown too impatient for buttons and ripped the shirt from her body. When had she ever felt such need? Now *that* was something she regretted not remembering.

You could always make a new memory.

No. Get dressed and get out.

Chagrin and agony filled his groan.

"What's wrong?" she asked.

"I must have taken my shirt off before the cuffs. I can't get it on now."

She reached for the pocketknife. "Raise your arm," she instructed, all doctorly and so professional. Yeah, professionally cutting off this man's shirt. She pried out the blade and cut from sleeve to hem.

Afterward, Owen reached for the buttons and fabric of her shirt, while her hand dangled from the cuff. "It's only fitting I cover you up," he said.

Her breath stuck in her chest when his fingers brushed against her skin as he did up the top button. She could barely breathe as he reached the last remaining button. The sleeve of her right arm flopped between them, the fabric ripped and torn to accommodate the handcuff. His left sleeve was also torn from end to end. A damning testament to their craziness the night before.

The evidence of her need for him made her feel vulnerable and defenseless. Stella hated feeling so weak.

"It's going to be okay, Stella," he said.

Her breath left her in a whoosh. It was exactly the right thing to say. She nodded, suddenly feeling not so alone. "Kiss me."

His head lowered and then his lips brushed across her lips in a slow, sensual caress. "I woke up wanting you, and that has never gone away," he said against her mouth, and her knees began to shake.

"Our bodies remember what our minds don't," she uttered.

He tongued the seam between her lips and her mouth parted. He gently entered her mouth, and their tongues met and slid against each other. She breathed him in, sunshine and cedar, and she breathed him in some more.

She lifted her arms to link them behind his neck, but the weight of his arm pulled at her elbow and broke the sensuous spell around them. He dropped a kiss on her cheek and rested his chin on the top of her head. Stella let her head fall against his chest and closed her eyes. Their breathing and the hum of the blower unit were the only sounds.

"You want to go out?" he asked. "I'm only here for a few days, but…"

She pulled away to look up into his hazel eyes, more a playful green now than brown. "Out? Like on a date?"

A knock sounded at the door and they broke apart, only to be slapped against each other once more. "We gotta get out of these cuffs," he said.

"I don't want anyone to see us like this. It's probably housekeeping. I'll just tell them to go away."

She padded to the door, Owen, of course, on her heels. "Hi, uh, we're good. We don't need anything," she said, trying to inject a note of cheerfulness into her voice.

"Stella? Stella Holbrook?"

A wave of alarm plunged through her. Beside her, Owen stiffened.

"It's Larissa Winston. From last night. Is Owen with you?"

The warnings from the three notes flashed through her mind.

You're in danger.

Only trust Owen.

Don't trust Larissa Winston!

Everything they'd written to themselves was coming true.

4

"DID SHE SAY LARISSA?" Stella whispered, just to double check that she'd heard correctly.

"The woman from the note?" Owen whispered.

Stella pressed her ear against the door. She heard the woman talking in a raised voice with the housekeeper. "I need you to open the door. I think my friends are hurt."

"If this isn't your room, I cannot open the suite," the housekeeper replied.

Stella squeezed her eyes shut. *Thank you, rules.*

"Something could really be wrong. Do you want that on your conscience?" Larissa said.

"Well…"

Sweat broke out along the back of Stella's neck. "We've got to get out of here." But she didn't move. Couldn't. She ran through her medical-school mantra in her mind. *Detach. Focus on moving forward. Know what you're doing.*

Owen backed away from her, and the slack in the chain between them leveled. "I'm not the one wasting time listening at doors."

Her mouth fell open. "What?"

"Stop checking out my body and hustle." He tugged her to his duffel bag and stuffed what he could inside.

Her entire body stiffened. "I'll show you hustle." She dragged him behind her to the balcony. Maybe they could hide out there if this Larissa person managed to get the housekeeper to key the enemy into their suite. Stella plucked up the notes that she could reach on their way, and spotted her slip-ons. *Yes!*

They'd left the drapes open when they'd checked the Dallas skyline. Owen pressed the Close button and the drapes began to move. "It will provide us cover," he told her. "Move. Try to tap into your survival instinct."

Jerk. She'd spotted a few jerky moments earlier, but pegged that as banter. Now she knew it was part of his personality. But his words got her moving. Stella crossed the threshold with Owen right behind her. He ushered her to the side so they'd be blocked from anyone entering the room. Plastered against the balcony wall, she strained to hear if the door inside their suite had been opened. Only Owen's breathing and the call of a lonely bird interrupted the silence. Then, *click*!

"Someone just opened the door," she whispered.

Owen scoped out the ground below them. They might be on the second floor, but it was a long way down. "Only way out of here," he said. Then Owen tossed his duffel bag over the railing.

She backed away from him, palms out. "Wait a minute."

He pulled her the three quick steps toward the railing. "If I'm going over, then *you're* going over."

"Do you know the probability of breaking your arm or your leg from a fall at this height?"

He kicked his leg up and straddled the railing. "Do you?"

"Well, no, but— Whoa!"

Owen gripped her hips, his fingers digging into her

skin. Then he lifted her up and over. "Don't worry. I do this all the time. Grab the post and wrap your legs around it. Then shimmy down."

Her fingertips dug into the railing until she found the post by feeling with her feet. One of her shoes fell off, making an icky plopping sound when it hit the concrete. *That could be my head.*

"If you fall, aim for the grass. Not the sidewalk."

"Thanks. That's very helpful," she said between gritted teeth. Stella worked her way down the railing post, giving her inner leg muscles the workout of a lifetime (though she suspected they'd also received a workout last night). Then she shimmied like no one had ever shimmied before.

"You got it, Doc. But can you hurry it up a bit?"

Why had she thought he had a killer bedside manner? She must have been delusional. At least she didn't have to wobble down the railing post barefoot holding a pair of cowboy boots like Owen. It would have made the trek downward much tougher. *Good. He deserves it.*

About two feet off the ground, she loosened her grip and allowed herself to free-fall to the grass.

When Owen reached the ground, he grabbed her by the shoulders and yanked her into the shadows of the brush, where she fell across his lap. Stella tried to scramble away, but he put a finger across his lips, and she nodded. See? She did have a survival instinct.

Above their heads she heard voices followed by footsteps and finally the closing of the balcony door.

Her shoulders sagged in relief. They were safe. "I cannot believe you tossed me over the balcony like that," she whispered. "What if I had fallen?"

"I would have let go and you could have landed on top

of me. I'm happy to cushion your fall, Doc." He wiggled his hips. He was cushioning her right now.

"You were above me," she pointed out.

"I'm heavier."

"That's not how gravity works."

He winked at her. This was the guy she'd chosen last night? Really?

"If you're done riding around on my buckle, I could put on my boots."

She shoved off him. *Detach. Detach. Detach.* "I think there's a park not too far from here. To the south."

"Good idea. You grab your shoe and I'll grab my bag. Ready?"

She nodded and he gave her hand a squeeze.

"Go!"

They sprang into action, slowing only so she could slip on her shoe and he could grip the handle of his duffel bag. The fingers of their cuffed hands twined together as they ran along the sidewalk surrounding the courtyard and out into the parking lot. They moved together as one, but Owen was in a lot better shape than she was. Five minutes into their sprint, Stella began to suck in breath and her pace slowed.

"I know you want to check out my ass, Doc, but we need to hurry now," Owen called over his shoulder.

"For the last time, I am not scoping out your ass." She had, but that was definitely over. For sure. But his words did add more angry energy to her stride, and soon they were crossing through traffic and ducking into the tree-shaded park.

She'd never been so happy to see a wide-open iron gate. Although the park wasn't busy, several office workers dressed in business suits and heels were enjoying the sun during a break in their busy day. Surely no one would try to confront them here, out in the open, and with witnesses.

Owen slowed the NASCAR-type speed, probably so they wouldn't draw attention from the others milling around, and led her to a red-painted park bench. She plopped down on a piece of rough-hewn wood, gulping in air and trying discreetly to rotate her feet in an effort to ward off any cramps in her calves. She'd start cardio training tomorrow. No later than Monday.

Owen didn't even appear all that winded. Must have been all the running and jumping and hauling of equipment. He was probably the kind of guy who called other guys *dude* or *bro*. Cowboy boots and handcuffs? What the hell had she been thinking? Exactly the kind of reckless and wild guy she'd never go for in a million years.

Except last night, a tiny voice inside her head taunted. Those tiny voices needed to mind their own damn business.

"It's okay if you want to freak out."

"I don't freak out. I never freak out."

"I think in this situation, you're allowed to freak out."

"Thanks for the permission."

"Not permission. I'm freaking out, too. It would be nice to have some company."

She smiled. Right, that's why she'd chosen him. Because he made her laugh.

A person could never count on autumn in Texas. Temperatures could hover in the high eighties or drop down to the cool forties. Today the sun shone brightly over her head, a gift before winter truly took over. But Stella couldn't admire the tiny park they'd found. Instead she willed her heart rate to even out because who knew what they'd be doing next? More running, probably.

Owen stretched out his long, jeans-clad legs beside

her. She had to hand it to the man. In less than two minutes he'd managed to annoy her so much she'd scrambled over a second-story balcony. A real accomplishment because she never let anyone goad her into losing her cool. A skill she'd learned from both her parents and received praise for from her professors at— Wait a moment...

She twisted in the seat to face him. "Were you being a jerk back there because you knew I'd respond better to that?"

His eyes widened. "Who, me?" His voice was all innocence and confusion.

"Don't mess with me. You figured me out." Which was actually kind of impressive. Her dream was to work as an emergency room doctor, and a good portion of the battle in the ER was gaining the trust of scared patients so they'd focus not on the injury or the pain but on healing. A portion of the battle she'd never really mastered. In a word, her bedside manner *sucked*.

But with just a few (irritating) sentences, Owen had gotten her to stop worrying about handcuffs and people chasing them, and instead on getting out of the hotel room to safety. There was more to this guy than a great set of abs and a smile that made panties melt. He—

Nope. Not interested in hidden depths. Or layers. Surface emotions only, thank you. The man beside her was gorgeous, yes. Clearly she'd hit the sexual jackpot last night, but that was it. *Take the money and run.*

"If it makes you feel any better, it wasn't hard figuring you out," he told her with a sexy shrug of his shoulders. "Prickly people are the easiest."

Stella stiffened. "I'm not prickly."

He flashed her a look.

"They're the easiest because prickly people never see themselves as prickly. That's why you get a response out of them when you give it right back. They're outraged someone could be so…prickly."

Stella opened her mouth to argue, and then quickly shut it. "You realize you put me in a no-win situation just now. If I argue, then I'm somehow proving I'm prickly. But if I agree…"

"Then you're admitting you're prickly. Honestly, it was easy. I spotted flashes of it in the bathtub this morning."

She would have complimented him on his approach, but the man beside her in no way needed any kind of encouragement. Girls had probably been sharing their dessert with him in the school cafeteria since the fifth grade. As teenagers, those same girls probably couldn't wait until Sadie Hawkins dances to snag this guy. "Any-way…thanks," she finally mumbled. Because not saying anything at all would be…prickly.

He gave her a wink. "All part of the job," he said.

"Oh, yeah, you're a first responder. So am I. Well, I will be when I finish med school."

"Ahh," he said, leaning against the back of the park bench. "That explains it."

"Explains what?"

"The God complex."

Stella cleared her throat. "You do realize the immediate crisis is over? You don't have to try to keep getting a rise out of me. And you're a first responder to the ladies, I bet. 'Let me help you while I look deeply into your eyes.' Does this hot-fireman routine get you a lot of play? Let's focus on our next plan. Maybe one that doesn't involve scrambling over balconies."

"You think I'm hot?"

She shook her head, and then looked over his shoulder to watch the sunlight play along the fall colors of the leaves. "I spoke a whole lot of words right there. Sentences that became a paragraph, even, and all you got out of it was that I may, or may not, find you hot?"

But Owen just smiled. "I'm just going where your words, sentences and paragraph lead. Besides, a man's gotta take what he can."

She rolled her eyes at that. "Somehow I don't think you're doing too badly in that area." Exhibit one—they were handcuffed together. Exhibit two—they'd been naked. Exhibit three—handcuffed together naked in a bathtub. "Okay, so who are you and what did you do that would put me in danger?"

His brows lifted. "Me? Why does it have to be me that put us in danger?"

Stella made a snorting sound. "I'm in med school, and as I have no radioactive spiders in the lab, it has to be you."

"I'm a firefighter. I don't even live in Dallas. It's not me."

Panic began to bubble, and her stomach clenched. She was due a freak-out, really. Honestly, she'd never experienced one, never needed to until now, but if waking up with no memory, naked and handcuffed to a stranger, didn't earn her one, she didn't know what would.

Instead Stella took a deep breath and began to follow the routine she'd developed in her sophomore year of college when she'd committed to following her parents into the medical field.

Don't react—detach. She shoved away all the panic and nervousness and fear until she felt nothing at all.

Replace emotions with knowledge. They had a lot of different facts, but not a lot of story.

Break it down—each step is one shift closer to your goal. Work the problem methodically.

"I picture two scenarios."

He lifted his arm and the chain dangled between them. "If you can figure this out, you should go into writing mysteries."

"Or maybe forensics." She shook her head. No, Stella craved the pace of the emergency room. "All right— scenario one. We've been mistaken for other people, and those people are tangled up in something really dangerous. Maybe they gave us their room last night to throw the bad guys off the scent. That explains the handcuffs. And why we were naked—a lot more difficult for us to run."

"What about the memory loss?"

Her shoulders sagged. "Yeah, that's where this pass-off-to-the-bad-guy scenario goes off the rails."

"You had another idea?" he prompted.

"We were drugged. It's not too far out of the realm of possibility. We could stop off at the hospital to draw blood and have it tested. The news is full of lowlifes drugging other people's drinks. Or someone wanted us loopy to rob us—my purse. It's not here."

"Maybe we stuffed it in the duffel." Owen rooted around inside his bag, but eventually he shook his head. "Nothing."

Stella rubbed at her temples in a weak attempt to stave off a pounding headache. She would have thought whatever illegal narcotic they'd been given would have caused a headache, but no. It was her own ridiculous emotions.

Don't react—detach.

"I think the notes have to do with me. Sort of," Owen said.

She rounded toward him. "I knew it."

He shook his head. "I'm, uh…"

"What?"

"I'm kind of…"

"What?"

The delectable skin she must have caressed with her lips and tongue last night reddened. "I'm kind of writing a book."

So the firefighter had a dream. That was kind of sweet. Nope. No, Stella wouldn't like anything about him. *Don't make this special. Don't romanticize him. He doesn't even live in Texas.*

She hadn't even begun the most demanding and challenging part of her path to becoming a doctor. She'd worked too hard to see everything derailed right now. And this sexy man beside her would definitely be a derailer.

"Why would you be embarrassed by that?"

He shrugged.

"Now look who's prickly." He only flashed her a crooked half smile. "Not even going to argue with me about it?"

"That's the thing. Nonprickly people can handle being called prickly." Then his smile faded. "Those note cards could have been some plot points and—"

"And me, being me, would have offered my own suggestions. So that explains the notes. What about the cuffs?"

He angled his head toward her.

"And the bathtub?"

He angled his head again, and Stella sighed. "Lust."

"That would be my guess. Of course the cuffs could also be part of my own self-preservation. I am attached to you," he said.

Something inside her stirred. This was the kind of man who put the safety of others first. A person who charged headfirst into a fire when other people ran off screaming.

Don't make him into a hero, Stella. Okay, the guy could be a hero, just not *her* hero. Thoughts like that were dangerous. Her ideal partner was someone like her dad, stable and supportive to both wife and daughter. Not an adrenaline-loving firefighter who would probably end up on a gurney in her hospital.

"Maybe that's what we should focus on first. Getting unattached. I'm sure there's any number of videos on the internet that could demonstrate how to get out of hand-cuffs. I'll just, oh, grrrr…"

"What is it?" he asked, his body alert, his eyes search-ing.

"I don't have my phone, either. I must have left it in my purse. Along with my car keys. The trifecta: no purse, no phone and no keys."

He shifted and dug his phone from the pocket of his jeans. "Good thing I, uh…"

"What?"

He showed her a dead screen. "No battery left."

"I have a charger in my car, not that it would help much. Something keeps bothering me about that last note."

"The one about Larissa?"

"Exactly. If those were plots for a book, how does she fit in?"

He rubbed the bridge of his nose. "Maybe scrambling over that balcony wasn't the best idea. Now I'm wonder-ing what would have happened if we'd calmly talked to her. After all, we're trusting ourselves—the same people who got us handcuffed."

And naked. And in a bathtub. He scored points for not mentioning that. He also scored points for making a pretty damn insightful observation. "Did we just run away from the one person who could have given us in-formation?"

"I think we should go back," she said. "If those notes are real, whoever is chasing us is probably long gone by now. If those cards are nothing more than notes for a book, then we can go back and get my stuff from the room. We either completely overreacted or should cautiously approach."

"I'm going with cautiously overreacted," he said, and she giggled.

When was the last time she'd giggled? When she was twelve? Thirteen?

Owen reached for his wallet and opened the leather flaps. "I don't see the room key. Wait…" He reached into his back pocket and pulled out a small leather case. Owen flipped it open and a plastic tab with a magnetic strip slipped out.

"Woo-hoo. That must be the key," she said. "Finally, something good."

"Waking up with a beautiful woman in my arms is always good."

She held out her hand. "See that? Completely steady. I could perform surgery. You don't have to try to get a rise out of me with flattery."

"I wasn't."

Stella hadn't meant to meet the pull of his gaze, but she did. Her mouth dried and she swallowed. Hard. Something tingly fluttered to life inside her. The rugged firefighter with a secret yearning to write drew her. A powerful and compelling temptation.

"Ready?" he asked.

Actually, she was.

Oh, wait, he meant returning to the hotel to retrieve her things. "It's going to be pretty interesting walking through that high-class hotel handcuffed together."

He shook his head. "Not sure the good people of the Market Gardens are ready for that."

"I have an idea. Can you bear holding my hand again?"

"I think I can manage that," he said, not hiding a grin.

He twined his fingers through hers.

"Maybe people will just think we're holding hands and won't even notice the cuffs and chain."

"Yeah, that's what I was going for," he told her, his voice dry.

They walked together along the winding path that twisted through the park—no more running. No one seemed to pay them much attention except a city worker minding the parking meters. The poor lady actually did a double take, then rolled her eyes and returned to work with a heavy sigh.

Stella didn't remember being in the Market Gardens, other than waking up in a guest bathroom and climbing over a balcony. Although she'd walked through this lobby last night, this morning the grand entrance was a brand-new experience, and it was stunning—everything an art-deco interior should display. Gorgeous wallpaper printed with chevrons, funky hardwood floors in geometric patterns and stunning bay windows. All the furniture and frames along the wall were vibrant and of nontraditional materials. "Wow. Just wow," she said, running her fingers through the water of the lobby fountain.

"I know how to treat a lady," he said with a wink.

"Does that charm usually work?"

He gave her the side eye. "Worked with you last night."

Stella swallowed a cough, and he pressed the Up button for the elevator.

A tiny tremor of apprehension snaked through her stomach when the *ding* announced their arrival on the second floor.

What were the chances they were in true danger? They'd found a reasonable explanation for almost every question they'd awoken to.

The warning notes *were* probably the book project Owen wanted to write—the one snag was Larissa.

More than likely, Larissa was someone they'd met the night before and they'd simply woven her into the story. They could even have mentioned where they were staying to her the night before, and she'd decided to pop in for coffee. Their memory loss could be explained by a truly heinous person drugging their drinks for his or her own sinister reasons.

Or they'd simply found easy explanations that didn't actually apply, and they were about to face a person with a knife or a gun or—

The hallway was empty.

She squeezed Owen's fingers. "All good."

"Were you worried?" he asked.

"Not at all."

His soft chuckle told her he didn't quite believe her. He faced her. "You don't have to do this, Stella."

"What do you mean?"

"We can go right back to the lobby. Ask for someone to get your purse. There are a few tricks to release the lock on the cuffs I can try and then…"

"Then?" she asked, her heartbeat quickening.

"We go. Forget this ever happened."

"Is that what you want?"

5

"Do I want to forget this ever happened?" His hazel eyes met hers. For one beat. Two. Then he focused somewhere above her shoulder. "You. This. It wasn't part of the plan."

"Well, it's good one of us was responsible and planned to wake up handcuffed to a complete stranger in a bathtub."

He chuckled, and the sound of it rolled down her back like a sensual caress. His gaze connected with hers again. His breath came out in a heavy sigh. "No. I'm not ready to let you go."

His words wrapped around and warmed her. "Let's check out the room, then."

They walked to their suite from the night before. With a swipe, the lock released and they were inside.

Owen smiled down at her. "We'll have to search the room for anything that might clue us in to where we were last night. Even the trash can." Then he swung the door wide.

They were in the suite, but the housekeeper had been there first—and not just to check on their well-being at Larissa's insistence. The bed had been made and the trash emptied, and the piney scent of cleaner filled the air.

"Do you see my purse?" she asked, scanning the delightfully opulent suite.

Owen shook his head, and they marched across the sitting area to check out the bedroom and the bathroom. "Looks like it's ready for the next occupant."

"And that would mean housekeeping would have my stuff."

With a nod, he faced the door.

"Wait." She angled her head toward the bathroom. "Quick stop there first."

Five minutes later and after one last scan around the beautiful suite she couldn't remember enjoying the night before and didn't have time to admire now, they raced into the hallway to try to spot the person who'd cleaned their room. But no housekeeping cart blocked their path in either direction.

"We'll have to go down to the lobby and talk to someone," Owen said.

Luckily they had to wait behind only one other couple at the front desk, but that didn't stop a few passersby from flashing an odd look at the couple joined together by handcuffs. The attendant was helpful and friendly, but the housekeeper who'd cleaned their room had taken the rest of the morning off for an emergency at home and wouldn't be back for several hours. The desk clerk assured them that when the purse was found, it would be stored in the safe for them.

Owen and Stella left the hotel through the grand entrance, the sliding doors swishing closed behind them. They stood silently watching cars and taxis drop off hotel guests in the circular drop-off.

"Okay, new plan," Owen said. "My grandpa was a huge woodworker back in the day. He had a shed in the backyard with a ton of tools my grandmother hasn't been able to part with. With his old setup, we can at least break the chain. Then work on the cuff later."

"Done," she said, and they took off for the parking lot.

"There's my truck." Owen pointed to a beat-up pickup, which at one time might have been navy blue but now was a dull gray. The prime of its life had passed at least a decade ago. Maybe two.

She kind of liked the dented and rusted wrecker. Made her think of long drives on dusty country roads in the summer with the windows down. Being a city girl through and through, Stella had never indulged in something so rustic, but it did seem a shame to have missed such a simple pleasure with the wide-open spaces practically in her backyard. Or maybe it was the hunk of temptation trapped beside her that forced her to daydream of things like tire swings over lakes and sunsets on rutted roads.

Owen the Tempter headed for the driver's side, while she aimed for the passenger's. They cut each other off, and she slammed into his side, her hand bracing on the hard contour of his ass. Stella dropped her hand in a rush. Touching him made her fingers tingle.

"That's not going to work," he said as they returned to their original factory settings—her on the left and him on the right.

She lifted her cuffed hand, and the chain jingled. "This will make driving awkward, too. Your arm will have to cross the steering wheel, and I'll have to sit at an odd angle. I could drive."

He shook his head.

"You're not one of those people who gets weird about others driving your truck?"

"Only about getting to my destination in one piece. The truck has developed a few…quirks."

She raised a brow.

"She only starts in Neutral."

Of course his truck was a woman. Probably ran like a dream for the man.

"The speedometer is a liar. Don't trust it. Ever. Oh, and you can't turn on the blower when she's accelerating. Or the windshield wipers. Or probably the radio."

She held up her hands and laughed. "Okay, I get it. You drive. I'll just hold my arm weirdly across my chest. I'll think of it as a kind of Pilates."

"What?"

She shook her head. "Never mind. Driver's side it is."

He unlocked the door and she hopped into the cab, not trusting the rusting running board. She scooted across the quilt-covered seat, and Owen followed her inside. His truck smelled like him, woodsy and enticing man, but she resisted the urge to breathe in too deeply. A pair of rugged hiking boots rested on the floor of the passenger side, and she imagined Owen didn't care much about the appearance of his vehicle because he spent so much time outdoors.

"What's your car look like?" he asked after the truck roared to life in, yes, Neutral.

Stella made a big show of fastening her seat belt. "Um, maybe you could just drive around in the parking lot, and if I see it, I'll point it out."

He angled his head toward her. "Don't you think it would be faster if we were both looking for it?"

She shook her head.

"What's the big deal?"

Stella sighed. "Okay, it's a red minivan."

"A what?"

"You heard me. Take your average mom-mobile, dial it up a few soccer balls and cups of ground-in cereal on the floor mat, and you have my car. I'm talking roof rack, sliding doors and a partially peeled off I'm Proud of My Honor Student bumper sticker. That adhesive is strong."

Owen's shoulders began to shake with laughter. "Why are you driving that?"

"I'm in med school. I'm not turning down free transportation. It was my mom's car before she got something cool."

Damn but his smile was charming, almost charming enough to make her forget how embarrassing her car could be. "I think I need to see you drive it to really get the full picture."

Yeah, almost enough. Stella shrugged. "Believe me, I've heard every joke possible since I inherited the thing. Of course it's all funny until someone wants to move."

"And when you need to take your fellow students to the intramural field."

"We wiped the plate with the law students," she joined in, because she could take a joke. Nope, not prickly at all.

"Maybe you could take me for ice cream later."

"Only if you're good."

"Oh, I aim to please."

And with that sexy promise, every nerve tingled and fired up to full attention. No, no, no. *Lead this conversation into some other direction.* Hadn't she already gone through the "he's not your type" conversation with herself?

"You a big camper?" she asked as they pulled onto the highway, remembering the boots. Excellent. Nothing sexy or enticing about camping. Bugs in her mouth, sleeping on the ground, and don't get her started on venturing off into the woods with a roll of toilet paper. In fact, she couldn't think of anything worse than camping.

A wide smile crossed his handsome face. "I go camping every chance I get. Living in Colorado makes it easy. Always another river to raft or bluff to hike. Sometimes I look out over the mountains, up at the blue skies that stretch out as far as I can see, and I can't believe I get to live in so much beauty."

"Hmm."

His gaze narrowed. "What?"

"Why, Owen, maybe it's the writing thing, but I do believe you have a bit of poetry in your soul."

He shuddered beside her. "Don't tell my sisters."

"How many do you have?"

"Three."

All that sisterly insight probably just made the man all the more lethal to womankind. "Not to worry. Your secret is safe with me."

"I've never had a secret from them. They can ferret out anything."

She pointed to the forming red ring around her wrist from the handcuffs. "Well, you never had me on your team before." And she'd just ignore the wave of warmth that crested inside her after that cheesy sentiment she'd just blurted out.

Actually, she'd never been part of a team, either.

"You mentioned you were in town for a family thing. Did your family move here from Colorado?"

He shook his head. "No, I'm Texas born and bred. I'm only visiting for my grandmother's birthday."

"So how'd you end up in Colorado?"

His hands tightened around the steering wheel, and the muscles of his jaw clenched and unclenched.

"Sorry, that was too personal…" Her words trailed off to silence. So his family was a nightmare or something bad had happened. Or both. And Owen clearly didn't want to talk about it.

"You camp?" he asked after a few minutes of silence.

Not if she could help it. "When the mood strikes."

"The trails around Saddlehorn are amazing, and…"

Owen shared some of his experiences hiking in the canyon country area with so much enthusiasm, Stella was almost ready to ditch her Wi-Fi and running water. Almost. After fifteen minutes he started down the ramp off the interstate.

"I've done nothing but talk," he said as he turned left and then right into suburbia.

"You're easy to listen to," she reassured him, surprised how much she enjoyed not having to talk. Or voice an opinion. Or give a diagnosis. The past few months of rounds had been nothing but that, waiting for the resident to pounce on any mistakes. Or dissecting her fellow students' analyses for errors.

Being with Owen was surprisingly easy. Relaxing. And, well…really nice. When she discounted the memory loss, handcuffs and acute embarrassment of wearing those cuffs in public.

He pulled up to the curb and parked his truck in front of a beautiful Tudor Revival home in the historic East Dallas area. Delightfully steep-roofed and half-timbered, the place invited lazy days of reading and discovering secrets. Homes like this always had secrets.

"No one should see us if we go through the side," Owen said, angling his head to draw her attention to an iron gate.

Something squeezed together in her stomach.

Owen didn't want anyone to see them together. Had all that warmth-inducing team-talk rattled him? Or maybe her questions about his personal life had prompted him to put distance between them.

What was so wrong with her that he didn't want a repeat of last night? One that they'd both remember?

She stamped that confidence-destructive question right out of her mind. Ugh, and contradictory much? There was nothing *wrong* with her. Just like there was nothing *wrong* with him. They just weren't *right* for one another.

He stepped out of the truck and held the door open until her feet hit the concrete. He closed the door quietly, and the two of them darted across the yard to the side of the house. Her heart raced and she was panting again. Okay, clearly she wasn't cut out for a life of crime. She could barely sneak into his grandparents' house without her flight instinct taking up firm residence.

The side gate had a touchpad lock, and after Owen pressed in a four-digit code, the latch released. Of course the iron creaked and groaned on its hinges when he pushed the door open, no matter how slowly he tried to do it.

"Open it quick. Like you're ripping off a bandage," she suggested.

After another ear-splitting screech, Owen did just that, and they slinked inside. Stella gasped as she rounded the corner of the house. The entrance hid a beautiful New Orleans–style tiled courtyard with checkerboard grass and flagstone pavers. She grabbed Owen's arm. "Wow."

Stella didn't know where to look first. The nineteenth-century-inspired limestone fountain with its vineyard grapes carved into the stone caught her attention first. The gorgeous bricked outdoor fireplace surrounded by curved rocking chairs also drew her attention. Several unique sitting areas were tucked throughout the yard. She'd been right. This house would have been her childhood dream. The place would be a joy in any season. Stella imagined her girlhood self exploring all the nooks and crannies or reading and dreaming of faraway lands in one of these sitting areas.

Her steps slowed. She wanted to take it all in, and lifted her hand so the water from the fountain could trickle over her fingers. "This is gorgeous."

Owen halted. His brow furrowed and he viewed the yard with one long panoramic glance. "If you like this kind of thing." Then he shrugged, pivoted and returned to marching her across the paving stones. *Yeah, I know you're in a hurry.*

Stella almost sputtered. "You prefer the untamed wilderness?" she asked his back. But of course he did. This man was the very picture of uncultivated. Which for some reason made her mouth dry. Kissing him had to have been like that. Fierce and passionate with no plotted course.

Whereas she was all about the cold facts.

But opposites attract, taunted some irritating and long-forgotten piece of dating advice. No, opposites didn't attract. They met and exploded, then burned out, leaving a whole lot of destruction in their wake. She's witnessed that phenomenon herself no less than six times since entering med school. Colleagues who fell hard for someone and either flunked out or pulled out of school. That wouldn't be her.

What Owen had referred to as a shed was more like a workshop. It was beautifully timbered to match the house. Someone had put a lot of thought and care into the construction. A bank of hinged windows and two wide double doors welcomed Stella. As she stepped across the threshold and onto the wooden floor, it felt as if she'd crossed into another person's past. She caught the scent of wood shavings and stain, and took a deep breath.

Owen flipped a switch, and shop lights hummed on overhead, revealing a large wooden table, worn and aged. Generations of projects must have been created on the weathered surface, and she couldn't help running the palm of her free hand across its rough plane. Wood was stacked against the wall and above her head and scrapped in a barrel to the side. Shelves storing every kind of power tool imaginable lined one wall, while another wall had pegs for hand tools used to carve, cut and join.

"Bingo. I see some bolt cutters," she said, pointing to the tool suspended by a peg. "Your grandpa must have been very organized."

Owen nodded. "Everything had its place." He reached for the plastic-coated handle of the bolt cutters and placed them on the table. "I won't be able to use them with just the one hand, but these we can use to cut through the wrist cuff once we're apart. Can you spot a hacksaw?"

Stella scanned the rows of tools.

"There it is," Owen said, and grabbed the tension saw and a couple of pairs of safety glasses.

"Glad you play it safe," she said and helped him with the strap behind his head.

"Oh, I always play it safe," he told her. His knuckles brushed her cheek and then smoothed away her hair as he helped her with the glasses. His voice was a seductive purr, and predictably, her body responded with the tiniest of shivers. Okay, it wasn't tiny. The sensation rocked her entire body.

Was this some new tactic of his? Was he now drawing a sexual response from her for distraction? Or could the man just not help using his sex appeal? Or maybe she just couldn't help responding to even the smallest of his gestures. Or maybe it was all three.

Stella held her breath and mentally counted to five. "I think the glasses are secure," she managed.

A small smile tugged at the corner of his mouth and his hands fell away. "Gramps had a couple of sawhorses around here somewhere."

Had he just winked at her? No, had to be a trick of the safety glasses.

They found a sawhorse hanging from the wall on hooks. With a flip, he positioned one in front of them. He slapped his wrist on one side of the wooden horse and with a nod indicated she should do the same.

"I'm not sure how long this will take, but keep the chain taut." He rubbed the soft skin beneath the wrist cuff. "If it becomes uncomfortable, let me know and we can take a break. You're skin is so soft and delicate."

And his caress felt so tempting. No wonder she hadn't been able to fight this last night. Besides being mouth-wateringly sexy, Owen smelled amazing. And he had a sense of humor and a bedside manner that, well, made her want to get bedside with him.

He tugged the chain between them. "You ready?" he asked as he picked up the saw.

She nodded and he began.

A dark slithering mass caught at the edge of her peripheral vision. She turned her head and squinted her eyes, but…nothing. With a shake of her head, Stella resumed her focus on Owen's slow but steady progress with the hacksaw. His head was bent in concentration, and a beam of fall sunshine shafted through the windows and brought out the honey strands in his brown hair.

Honey strands? Really? Had she just gone there?

Owen was the perfect specimen to end the man-fast, but that's all it could ever be. Owen was simply not her type. This man was not for her after today.

Or tonight...

The flutter of movement along the wall grabbed her attention again. "Your family doesn't have a barn cat, does it?" she asked.

He shook his head. "No, my grandmother is allergic. Wait, I think. I. Got. It."

The chain linking them together broke apart. Their gazes met and they shared, *really shared* a smile. A smile she felt all the way to her currently curling toes.

His eyes narrowed and the green in Owen's hazel eyes darkened. She felt herself sway toward him.

A sliding and coiling thing slithered behind Owen. A chill ran down her back. She shouldered him out of the way and grabbed the nearest sharp object. A shovel. With a whack, she killed the snake that was about to strike Owen's calf.

"You're freaking fierce, lady," he told her, eyeing the cold-blooded would-be killer snake.

The shovel dropped from her fingers and clanged to the wooden floor. Adrenaline rushed and pumped through her body, and her arms began to shake. Stella braced her hands on her thighs, readying herself for the eventual crash of shock.

Talking had always seemed to help in the past. "I hate to kill any living creature, but I hate treating someone for a poisonous snakebite even more. That was a copperhead."

Owen hunkered down to examine the distinctive bands on the creature. "You're right. That means there might be more. No one's been out here in a while." He rubbed at the back of his neck. "If it makes you feel any better, I'll make sure the other snakes are taken someplace where they can live long and happy snake lives."

Relief chased away the last wave of adrenaline. "Told you your penis got off easy this morning," she teased.

His answer was a slow, rich chuckle, the kind that wrecked a woman's defenses and good intentions. *Her* defenses and good intentions. Stella brushed her sweaty palms down her leggings and straightened, needing not to feel so vulnerable.

"Thanks," he said. Just one word, but filled with some unidentifiable emotion. Owen's fingers curved around her shoulder. "You okay?"

She shrugged.

"Hey, I'm a firefighter. I know what it's like to deal with the aftermath of adrenaline."

She glanced up and searched his eyes. Concern dwelled in those hazel depths. "I'm good. Thanks."

There was no playful banter now. No suspicious self-preservation. She owed him more. She owed herself more. "I can separate myself from the emotion. I'm especially good at that, actually. It's just dealing with that crazy rush of adrenaline."

"I know exactly how to handle it."

"How?" she asked.

"You channel it somewhere else." His eyes lowered to her mouth.

Stella's breath hitched. He was gazing down at her like he wanted to devour her. She ached for the feel of his mouth, and her fingers drifted to her lips. His warm hand covered hers, drawing her fingers away. Then his mouth dropped to hers.

It was gentle. Exploratory. Like a first kiss. Which it was, really. No matter what had happened between them last night, *this*, this tug of awareness and want and need, *this* was new to her. And even though this man wasn't her type and wouldn't be in her life long, she could no longer fight the attraction that burned between them. She took her hand from his and molded it to his head, drawing him closer. Urging him to kiss her harder.

With a groan he gripped her hips and drew her flush against his body. She flattened herself along the strength of his chest and thrilled at the feel of the growing length of his cock.

Stella opened her mouth, and the sexy velvet of his tongue sought hers. She breathed in his outdoorsy, woodsy scent, felt her fill of the tight muscles roping his back and arms, and reveled in the sound of his labored breathing. *Exactly.*

She'd made his breath ragged. This sexy man wanted *her.* She hooked her leg around his hip and moaned as the hard ridge of him swelled between her legs.

Then a voice said, "I think Dad stored some coolers in the shed. Ahh—Owen? Is that you?"

6

LARISSA KEYED INTO the offices of PharmaTest and disabled the alarm, then sagged into the chair of her office. "Don't be too relieved. There are still two more people out there completely unaccounted for."

Talking out loud to herself was probably not a good sign, either. Still, she powered up the computer with a smile. Twelve and Ninety-Two were fine. They'd checked into a hotel last night, and although she'd missed them this morning, the pair had probably been at breakfast or something. After all, Ninety-Two's purse had still been there when the housekeeper opened the door to the suite.

When those four patients woke up this morning, other than the memory loss and anxiety reduction, any other effects of the drug would have worn off.

Her head fell back and Larissa blew out a heavy breath. Perhaps she'd blown everything out of proportion last night. And again this morning. Sure, the subjects had acted a little giddy as they'd signed their release forms and left the PharmaTest offices last night, but why had she been so worried they'd do something crazy? HB121 relieved pain. The drug aided in trauma. Some people even said it helped them think better and work out their problems.

So she'd found the first two patients. Sort of. Now on to Thirty-Five and Seventy-Eight. First item on the agenda: run a search on the internet for any people acting strange or unusual in the area. She scrolled through the search hits, but nothing stuck out other than the typical overnight Dallas shenanigans. Another average Thursday night.

Next Larissa moused over the local news sites, but there were only stories about a faulty tornado siren and upcoming high school and college football games.

That left the patient intake files. Larissa ran her fingers along the folders until she located the four in question. First up—subject thirty-five. Hayden Taylor. She'd listed herself as a student and given a local address. Volunteer seventy-eight, the man she'd left with, Larissa remembered was a documentary filmmaker from California.

Subject twelve was a firefighter from Colorado. The last volunteer, ninety-two, and the one who'd called the offices last night, lived right here in Dallas. The four of them had left PharmaTest together, which might mean some of them had left their cars in the lot. Grabbing her keys, Larissa trekked out to the parking lot.

A well-loved red minivan and a beat-up yellow sedan were the only other cars outside, and Texas license plates were affixed to both of them. Larissa trudged back into PharmaTest. She would leave notes on the windshields. Bingo!

Larissa dashed to the computer and printed off two notes with her contact information and a request to telephone or email her. Then she slid them under the windshield wipers. A huge gust of wind barreled down on her

as she raced back to office, and she had to fight to keep
her skirt from flying up over her head. And despite that
potential embarrassment, she blinked back happy and
relieved tears.

"Hello, Ms. Winston."

Larissa whirled around to see the oh-so-sexy Dr. Durant propped against the front desk. How long had he
been there? Had she just flashed the man her panties?
A flush stained his cheeks. A hue not normally present.

She gave him a half smile and made a show of locking the front door, trying to hide her shaking fingers. Dr.
Durant rarely showed up so early. She had thought she'd
have more time to sort things out.

He stood as she turned to face him. Tall and gorgeous,
the man wanted to make the world a better place. Ease
the pain and suffering of the hurting and injured. He deserved so much more than her shoddy efforts last night.
And her brushoff this morning.

"Since you couldn't get away earlier, I decided to bring
something to you. I remember how you, uh, you mentioned once… I brought you some cheesecake." He thrust
a small takeout container toward her.

If life had to be boiled down to one dessert that made
it worth living, that treat would be cheesecake. When
had she told him that? One, one-and-a-half years ago?
And he'd remembered?

She dragged in a breath. The back of her throat tightened and she pressed her lips together to hold back a
sniffle.

But he spotted the wetness on her cheeks and his gray
eyes narrowed. In two long strides he was at her side, his
large hands engulfing hers. "Larissa, what is the matter?"

The handsome doc never called her Larissa. Always
the formal and professional Ms. Winston. She began to

tremble and his thumb stroked her hand. Soothing her. It was the first time he'd ever touched her.

And the last.

What was the matter? *Everything.* She shook her head. "Nothing." Larissa forced a smile. "I'm fine."

"But you're crying."

His tender caring, his gentle caress…now? Finally? It was almost all too much. Larissa yanked her hands from his and moved past the informal lobby and toward the inner area where the patient lounges and rooms were located. "I have to straighten up."

"Of course. I'll help."

He'd never offered to help before.

"It's just busy work," she told him over her shoulder as she punched the key code and the lock unlatched.

"We're a team, right?"

Yeah, and she was the team member who'd dropped the ball. The heavy metal door slammed shut behind them and she was alone, truly alone with the only man who'd ever made her go weak in the knees. She forced herself to walk down the narrow corridor and escaped into the first patient sleeping room. This room had been assigned to one of the patients who'd bailed on her last night.

He followed her. So now she was alone. With Dr. Durant. Alone. In a tiny room filled by a bed. *Alone.*

"What normally happens in these rooms?"

Good. Focus on the routine. "The morning after the medication was dispensed to you, I would check your pulse. Listen to your breathing."

Dr. Durant extended his wrist, and her mouth gaped. She took his hand. His skin was smooth under her fingertips, and Larissa needed an extra moment to find his pulse. It beat steady and sure and…elevated?

"You're at one ten. That's a little high."

"My pulse is always a little high when I'm with you."

She'd just managed to get her mouth closed when he let loose another jaw-dropping statement.

"Maybe you should check my breathing," he suggested, and a blast of heat singed her down the middle. She'd never seen Dr. Durant dressed so casually. Jeans and a cotton button-down shirt. And never without his lab coat. Sometimes he even wore suits when he arrived at PharmaTest for presentations.

But today he was a different Dr. Mitch Durant. Not just in his early appearance or the way he dressed but also his whole demeanor toward her were different. Almost flirtatious.

"Aren't you going to check my breathing?" he asked as he plopped down on the bed.

Definitely flirtatious.

She flattened her palm against his chest, and he sucked in a gulp of air. The steady thump beneath her fingertips energized her. "Your breathing feels erratic."

His gray eyes met hers and Larissa struggled to read his thoughts. Her throat tightened with emotion. Was the man she'd longed for, daydreamed over, really here and giving her exactly what she wanted?

His hand covered hers over his chest. "I could be in some distress," he said, his tone grave.

She cupped his cheek and lowered her head to his. She explored his lips. Rubbed her mouth along his upper lip. His lower lip. Traced the seam with her tongue.

No response from him.

She pulled away. His eyes fluttered open, his irises dark.

"You have no idea how long I've wanted to do this," she admitted. Breathless. If she'd read his signals wrong and he rejected her now, she didn't care.

"I have some idea."

Then Dr. Durant took off his glasses.

He tossed them onto a small end table beside the bed. Dr. D—Mitch gripped her wrists and tugged her forward onto his chest. "I have to stop myself every damn day from driving over here to visit you. I ran out of convenient excuses over a year ago."

With a laugh, she tucked her hair behind her ears. "I had no idea."

He nodded. "I know. You never saw me."

She traced the solid angle of his jaw with her finger. "Oh, I saw you, Dr. Durant. Mitch."

His eyes squeezed shut. "You have no idea how long I've waited to hear you call me by my name."

"Mitch," she said again.

His long dark lashes fluttered open, and the joy and desire dwelling in the dark depths of his eyes made her mouth go dry. "What happens next with your patient? To me?" he asked, his hands stroking and rubbing up and down her back. His scent of sandalwood filled her nose and she breathed it in. Deep.

Larissa found it hard to concentrate. "I ask a series of questions."

"What are they?"

"You created them," she reminded him.

"Ask," he invited.

A delicious thrill of sensation rushed through her. She licked her lips. "How did you sleep?"

"Lousy."

His answer excited her beyond reason. Could *she* be the reason for his restless sleep? She'd suffered many a restless night due to the sexy research doctor.

"Are you under an unusual amount of stress?"

He nodded, and his hands lowered. Was Dr. Durant about to grab her ass?

"Why?"

Something dark and urgent burned in his gray eyes. "Because I realized this phase of the drug trials is nearly complete."

Her brow furrowed. "That's a good thing. HB121 will help millions of people all around the world. You're amazing."

"We're amazing. It took all of us to get this far. But once we're out of this phase of development, I may never see this incredible woman again, and it eats me up inside."

He cupped her butt then, and pressed her until she felt the force of his erection between her legs. Larissa began to tremble and she grew wet and needy. She straddled him then and through their clothes rubbed her clit against the hard ridge of his penis. She was done with being shy. His agonized groan was her reward.

He sunk his hands into her hair and drew her mouth down to his lips. His kiss was wild and wicked and so not what she'd imagined. His tongue darted inside her mouth, robbing her of anything other than need. Need for him.

He rolled her onto her back. How had he managed to do that on such a narrow bed? Her sexy doc was magic. He slid off her body until he knelt between her spread thighs. His hand kneaded up her legs, soothing her and making her tense at the same time. "I leave here and all I think about are these skirts you wear. They drive me crazy. You have amazing legs." He shuddered. "And then this morning, ahh, agony."

"Why?"

"Because when your dress flew up in the wind, I saw exactly what these skirts hide." His fingertips caressed her thighs and her legs began to tremble. Up, up, up his hands traveled until he found her panties. "And these…" He fingered the delicate red lace. "These almost killed me."

She lifted her hips. "Take them off."

Mitch didn't waste any time. He hooked his thumbs around the lace at her hips and drew the material down, revealing the most intimate parts of her to him.

He sucked in a breath. "You're the most beautiful thing I've ever seen. I've got to taste you."

Her eyes drifted shut at the image his words evoked. "Yes. Please."

His fingers were gentle as he played about the folds between her legs, and Larissa arched her back. "More," she urged.

His thumb centered on her clit, he circled around the delicate bud of nerves for a heartbeat, then off. On. Then off. Her toes curled into the blanket on top of the tiny bed. His thumb forged lower, slipping into her wetness.

Her voice became a whimper. "That feels so good."

"It's about to feel a whole lot better." His thumb slid inside her and her hips bucked. Then Larissa felt the wetness of his tongue above her knee as he teased the ticklish spot. His thumb alternated between orbiting her clit and sliding between her folds, and all the while his mouth dragged up her inner thigh, nearing her core.

Then his hand fell away. Her stomach hollowed and her shoulders sagged. Mitch gripped her around the ankles and hauled her legs behind his back. She was completely open to him now. She should feel vulnerable. Exposed. Instead she felt desired. He blew on her skin and a thousand tiny shivers erupted along the apex between her thighs. Her nipples puckered and her head wobbled from side to side.

Then he kissed her and drew her clit into his mouth. Teasing. Sucking. His fingers tweaked her folds and drew them apart, and he laved her with his tongue from clit to core. Her tortured moan tore through the tiny sleeping room. Larissa's legs dropped, and her heels dug into the thin mattress and her fingers molded to his head.

He slipped a finger inside. Then another. She rode his hand, aching for release. Mitch grazed her clit with his mouth, his teeth and his tongue each a different sensation that drove her closer and closer to the edge.

The sexy doctor added another finger and her entire body contracted. Mitch licked her clit until the waves of her orgasm ended. She felt weightless and pinned to the bed at the same time. Her hands fell to his shoulders and she drew him up her body.

"Mitch, I want you so much. Please."

"I don't have protection."

"It's okay. I'm on the pill."

The good-doctor-gone-bad flashed her a smile so sexy that she had to bite her lip. "You're sure?"

She nodded. "Yes, *now.*" Larissa hadn't meant to sound so insistent. She'd practically ordered the doctor to take her and—

He plunged his hard length inside until his sac hit against the sensitive skin between her thighs. He leaned his forehead against hers, his eyes so close to hers she couldn't focus. "You feel amazing, Larissa. Better than I ever imagined."

"You imagined this?"

"Every. Damn. Night." He punctuated each word with a thrust.

Larissa wrapped her legs behind his back again, locking her ankles. "Did you think about me doing that?"

"I hoped you would."

"What about this?" she asked and flexed her hips to meet his thrust.

He groaned and shook his head. "This is too good to have imagined."

She gripped his face and kissed his lips. "Go. Harder. Faster. Just make me come again." Larissa sucked his tongue into her mouth, and he began to thrust hard into her body. She gripped him tighter with her legs, her fingers digging into his skin.

He cupped her breasts between their bodies, tweaking her nipples through the material of her bra. Her muscles clamped around him, and with a groan, Mitch rode her orgasm until he exploded inside her.

His left shoe hit the ground, then the right. Dear God, she hadn't even let the man undress before she demanded he ride her. And she didn't give a damn.

They lay together, her dress bunched up at her waist and his pants partially pushed down his legs.

She almost giggled at the force of her need for him. This, this was what she'd been waiting for. "Better than I ever imagined," she murmured.

"Damn straight," he said, and pulled the blanket up over them. He tucked her against his side and kissed her temple, and she fell asleep against the man she'd only ever had in her dreams.

IN THE SHED, Owen shoved Stella behind his back in a protective gesture that was old-fashioned and kind of sweet. Stella blinked against the harsh sunlight peeking through the open door.

"Yeah, sis. It's me." His voice sounded resigned.

A bright smile pulled at the corner of their intruder's lips. An expression she'd spotted on Owen. "Is that a girl you're trying to hide behind your back? Not doing such a great job. No offense."

"Not hiding anyone."

"I killed a snake."

They spoke at the same time.

Owen's sister cocked her head. "Wait, are you kissing the exterminator?" Then her gaze lowered. "Holy shit, is that part of a handcuff you're wearing?" Her gaze shifted to Stella. "That you're *both* wearing? And what's wrong with your shirt? *Both* your shirts?"

"Uh…"

Owen's sister clapped her hands. "Oh, man, this story is going to be good. I'm getting the girls." The double door slammed back into place behind her.

"This is a disaster," she heard Owen mumble.

Stella's back stiffened. Okay, the man might not be her type, and it was clear he didn't think she was his usual kind of woman, either, but did he have to make it so obvious?

"What's the big deal?" she hissed, not able to mask a hint of defensiveness. "We're all grown-ups, after all. So we've been caught kissing. No biggie."

He rubbed the back of his neck. "You know in movies how the younger brother seems to have these wise older sisters looking out for him with the school bully or ready to dispense uniquely feminine dating advice so he brings the hardest-to-get girl to the prom?"

Stella nodded, because what else could she do?

He sighed. "I didn't have that kind of sisters. More like the constantly tormenting, let's watch him fail and laugh kind of sibs."

As an only child, this scenario sounded horrifying. "How many did you say you had again?"

"Three," he finally said. "That was Bethany, the oldest." Then he turned from her, his shoulders straightening. Bracing for battle? He marched toward the workbench and grabbed the bolt cutters. "Let's get these off quickly."

She followed and placed her arm on the table, palm up. She tucked her finger under the metal band and tugged it up to give him clearance. Owen slid the smooth, cold metal of the bolt cutter along her wrist, the blades sharp and ready. With one quick snip, the cuff split and she was free.

Stella rubbed the chafed skin that for some reason didn't hurt even a little, and enjoyed the pure joy of liberation. "Thanks. Okay, your turn. Hand them over."

The double doors swung open again and in the entry stood Bethany and another woman who shared Owen's and his sister's honey-highlighted hair. "Mom, Owen's brought a girl to Gram Gram's birthday party."

Gram Gram?

Stella stepped in front of the remnants of Owen's cuffed hand in a vain attempt at hiding the stupid thing. But she just drew attention to the damaged metal and appeared even guiltier.

"If I had a dollar for every time I was in handcuffs, I'd be able to retire," replied the woman at Bethany's side.

Stella gaped at her.

"You see?" Owen said. "Everyone in my family is a natural-born tormenter. That offense was intentional. So I guess I can't be too angry with my sisters. They come by it naturally. I've been completely desensitized by all the things my mom says."

She made a *tsk*ing sound and then rushed to his side. "You used to get so embarrassed. No offense, but it made you stronger." She kissed him on the cheek. "Glad to have you back, son." The older woman's voice caught. "Don't stay away so long next time."

Owen's arms wrapped around his mom's shoulders and he gave her a hug. Stella's throat tightened at the warm scene. For a moment she let herself miss her own parents.

How long had he been gone? Other than a little teasing, his family didn't seem to fall into the total-nightmare-must-escape category.

The big, strong firefighter acted like he had three tormenting sisters and an oversharing mom, but there was a lot of love in this family. And yet, he'd moved away... Why had he left?

"I won't," he assured his mother.

Although Stella had less than twenty-four hours worth of memories of the man, she knew he meant his promise. Something—or was it some*one*?—had kept him away, but maybe enough time had passed that he could come home.

"This is Stella..." His words trailed off as his eyes widened. He didn't know her last name.

She stuck out her hand, the red ring around her wrist apparent, the material of her shirt flapping. "I'm Stella Holbrook."

"Karen Perkins," his mom replied as she returned Stella's handshake. "Been dating long?"

She shrugged her shoulders. "Sometimes it feels like we just met yesterday."

Karen laughed and clasped Stella's hand. Tight. "I understand exactly what you mean. It's nice to always be discovering new things about a man. Keeps you on your toes. And makes it hot between the sh—"

"Mom," Owen groaned.

Owen's mother flashed her a warm smile. "I'm so glad you could make it for Gram Gram's birthday. Won't she be surprised? Owen's never brought a date to a family event before. You must be pretty special."

Wait a moment. He'd mentioned he was in town for a family thing. He'd taken her to his grandmother's home knowing that a whole houseful of relatives would be there. He might have practically dragged her across the lawn to avoid detection, but why bring her here in the first place? Why not just stop at any of the home improvement stores they'd spotted along the way?

"Did you drive down from Colorado with him?" his mother asked.

"Uh, actually I'm from Dallas."

"Really?" His mom's smile widened. "That's wonderful news."

Guilt thrummed through her. Oh, no, had she just given his family some kind of false hope that Stella might lure Owen back to Dallas? For her?

"I was just about to lay out some cold cuts and salad for a quick lunch. We'd love for you to join us."

"Well, I, uh…" she hedged. Why couldn't she dredge up some kind of plausible excuse? She was supposed to be quick on her feet.

Then Owen draped his arm around her shoulders. "We'd love to."

She blinked. Was this the same guy who'd referred to being caught by his sister a few moments ago as a disaster?

He angled his head toward the handcuff and chain still dangling from his wrist. "We'll just finish up out here."

"Yeah, not sure what Gram would say about that. C'mon, Bethany. You can help me set out the plates."

Owen's sister laughed. "Really? Set out the plates? No offense, but that's the excuse you came up with?"

Mrs. Perkins curved her hand on Bethany's shoulder

and turned the young woman toward the door. "Move it. Your brother wants to be alone with his girlfriend. My guess is, he's going to make sure she doesn't bolt for that ratty old truck of his."

The door shut behind them. Stella counted silently to three so Owen's family would be out of earshot. Then she rounded on him. "Are you crazy? I had almost three legitimate excuses lined up to get out of here, and then you blew it."

"Crazy? More like genius. I'm using you as a human shield against my sisters."

"Oh, please. Your family is great."

Owen shuddered. "I learned what a half nelson was from my sisters. As they performed it on me." But there was a smile in his voice as he returned to the worktable. He picked up the bolt cutter and attempted to hand it to her, but Stella reached for his hand instead.

"Owen, why am I here?"

"The tools are here."

She shook her head. "No. We could have stopped off at any hardware store. There are probably at least three between the hotel and here. We'd have gone our separate ways by now."

The bolt cutters clanked against the table as he dropped them. His gaze clouded and he frowned. He sucked in a breath and blew out the air, his cheeks puffing. "I guess I wasn't ready to go my separate way from you yet."

"Oh." Of all the answers she could have expected, that admission wasn't one of them. It left her a little…dazed.

"But you practically dragged me across the grass to get in here. I'm surprised you didn't hoist me over your shoulder, firefighter-style."

"We don't actually do that anymore. Smoke and heat

are really more dangerous the higher you hold a person. That's why in a fire you should crawl on the floor, get as low as possible."

She crossed her arms across her chest. "So you're saying you dragged me across the yard earlier because of your training? Like muscle memory?"

He shook his head. There was that half smile all the Perkinses seemed to share. He lifted his wrist. "You as buffer—yes. You as handcuffed buffer—no. Besides, I was in a hurry because I wanted to spend a little more time with you. Not more time with you *and* my family."

"Wow, you have a way of sucking the righteous indignation right out of a person."

"It's my superpower."

She would have gone with "sexy as hell" being his superpower. Drawing a woman's attention with a single glance. More powerful than common sense. Able to shatter a woman's romantic defenses in a single bound.

Stella slumped against the worktable, and Owen edged around to slump right beside her. She glanced over at him. "Are you worried? About last night? What we might have done?"

Owen shook his head. "My mom wasn't worried, and the plan yesterday was that I was supposed to sleep over at their house last night. I must have called so my parents wouldn't freak out when I didn't show."

"Do they still have your old bedroom?"

He tugged at the collar of his shirt. "Mom hasn't changed a single thing."

"That's kind of sweet."

By Stella's sophomore year in college, her mom had converted Stella's bedroom into a craft room. There was always the guest bedroom, but most of Stella's high school memories and memorabilia were boxed up and stacked in the attic, ready for when she wanted to claim it.

He stared straight ahead, his gaze unfocused. "They didn't understand my need to get out. I couldn't stay in Dallas."

The garden wasn't the only thing with secrets. Stella was growing more and more intrigued about the rugged man beside her. But she couldn't get any more involved with her one-night (maybe one-weekend) guy than she already was. She braced herself off the table and grabbed the bolt cutters. "C'mon, firefighter. You have a date with the shears."

He snatched his hand away. "Are you sure? Don't cut me."

She adopted her most reassuring expression and comforting voice. "Please. I'm a doctor. I won't just cut you, I'll do it with precision accuracy."

He plopped his arm on the sawhorse with a snort. "Had to pick one with sass."

He lifted the metal cuff and she slid the bolt cutters in place. With a single snap, she freed him.

"Damn. Not even a scratch," she said with faux complaint.

He squinted at his wrist then held out his hand to her. "Actually…I may see something there."

"And you need medical attention?"

"Maybe even a full examination."

She gripped his arm and examined the skin where the cuff had once been. Slight redness, maybe some bruising. "Does this hurt?"

"No. It's not numb, but it's as if I couldn't feel pain if I tried to hurt myself."

"But you winced when I touched the marks on your back."

"The marks you gave me?" he asked. Satisfaction punctuated his every word. "I winced because a gorgeous woman caressed the sex wounds she'd given me the night before."

Sex wounds? She dropped his hand. "You'll be fine."

"That's some pretty amazing bedside manner you have there, Doc."

Her gaze narrowed. Had he just challenged her? Stella reached for his arm. "Let me try this again." She gently ran her fingers down the sensitive skin of his palm. His fingers flexed at her slow and lazy touch. Had she read somewhere that the underside of the wrist was an erogenous zone? Didn't matter. She would make it one.

She raised his arm higher, until her breath teased the skin of his arm. She ghosted his wrist with her lips and smiled at his quick intake of air. "Does that hurt? Or are you almost numb?" she asked.

Owen shook his head. "Definitely not numb."

So pain receptors dulled, but pleasure sensors fully engaged. Interesting. She flicked her tongue against his heated skin. "How about now?"

"No." He swallowed. "I'm good."

"It's my medical opinion that I should continue my examination." If she'd watched this scene in a movie, it would have been cheesy as hell, but here, in the shadows of the shed, with the sexiest man alive, she felt bold and sensual. She liked teasing him. Liked that he liked it, too.

"If that's what the doctor orders."

She offered him a grave nod. "It's my professional medical opinion." Stella ran her lips slowly up his arm, and she couldn't help smiling as his hand fisted. "Most people call this the crease of your elbow, but its medical name is the cubital fossa." She kissed the skin she met there, and then licked him. He rewarded her with an agonized groan. That raw sound made her ache. All this for just a little play with an elbow? She was in trouble with this one.

Stella dropped his arm. "I think you're good."

He chuckled low in his throat, and the sound of *that* even made her nipples harden.

"Wow. That was hotter than I ever would have imagined." His gaze dropped to her lips. "I know why I left Colorado yesterday morning with one plan and woke up to something else."

"Why?"

"This." Owen's hands curved around her shoulders, and he tugged her against the rock-solidness of his body. His head lowered and his mouth grazed against hers. Then he settled his lips on hers, and her breath caught in her chest.

He traced the seam of her mouth with his tongue and then slid his lips along hers. Stella draped her arms around his neck. Her nipples puckered inside her bra and she rubbed her breasts against him to feel more.

His lips broke from hers and he rested his forehead on hers. "Ah, Stella. You're amazing," he told her, his breath ragged. "I could stay out here the rest of my days just kissing your lips."

She shot him a skeptical glance. "Just kissing?"

And yes, there was that sexy half grin in response. "Oh, I could fill the time with you, believe me." Then his expression grew serious. "It's going to be awkward as hell with my family, and I know spending Friday night with complete strangers wasn't your plan for this weekend."

She shrugged. "I can't remember what my plan was for the weekend."

He cupped her cheeks. "Just say the word and I'll

drive you wherever you want to go. I need to grab an intact shirt anyway."

Actually, that was exactly what she should tell him to do. Drive her back to her apartment. One of her roommates would let her in. Hell, one of them might know what she'd done last night. It made perfect sense.

She looped her arm through his. "I think I was promised lunch."

His shoulders relaxed and his sensual lips curved into a smile just for her. "You sure? My family will probably drive you nuts with their questions and their full-on intrusion into your life. No topic is safe."

Emotions were complicated and not to be trusted. She'd been taught to control them from an early age. But today, right now with this delicious man, what would be the harm in letting that tight control go for once?

"Are you kidding? I gotta see the house that goes with that garden."

7

THE HOUSE DID not disappoint. French doors led from the courtyard into a large and airy great room. She'd imagined something stuffy and maybe a bit formal to go with the Tudor Revival style, but the furniture was soft and inviting. Family pictures graced the walls, the mantel and the bookshelf...actually, every available space.

The ceiling soared high above her head, arched with cross-timbers and two beautiful stained-glass bay windows with stuffed cushioned seats, which invited a quiet conversation. Or a stolen kiss.

The great room opened into a large kitchen where Karen and Bethany and two other women who must be Owen's sisters were busy laying out cold cuts and sides. Karen rushed over to her as soon as they entered. "I've placed one of Charlotte's blouses for you in the hall bath if you want to freshen up before you meet the rest of the family."

With a grateful smile, Stella quickly ducked into the bathroom. She closed the door and hugged her arms around her waist, alone for the first time since...well, she didn't know how long. After splashing water on her face and smoothing her hair into some semblance of order, she removed her shirt.

Stella loved this little black-and-white top, but there was no saving it now. With a shrug, she tossed it into the trash. A folded lavender silk blouse waited for her on the counter. The cut was a little old-fashioned, but the fabric was soft and expensive, and Stella gratefully smoothed the shirt in place. With a deep breath, Stella twisted the knob and left her refuge to return to Owen's family.

In front of a roaring fire sat a nice-looking man who shared Owen's height and broad shoulders. The man's eyes were brown instead of hazel, but he had to be Owen's father. Beside him sat an older woman, a cane at her feet. This must be the Gram Gram everyone was talking about.

Owen's father stood as Stella entered, and he greeted her with a warm smile. She suspected the man would have preferred to meet her with a hug, he seemed so happy to see the both of them. "Welcome, come in."

"Stella, this is my dad, Roger."

"We're so glad you were able to make the trip down from Colorado," he said, his hand engulfing hers in quick shake.

"She's from right here in Dallas, honey," Karen called from the kitchen.

His big smile widened. "Even better."

Owen kneeled in front of the older woman still reclining in the overstuffed lounger, although she didn't appear to be happy about it. Her toes tapped against the hardwood floor and her fingers gripped the armrest like she'd propel herself to stand by force if she could.

"And this lovely lady is my grandmother, Charlotte Perkins."

"I'd greet you properly if the surgeon wasn't forcing me to sit in this chair."

"You'll be dancing in no time," he assured her. Owen glanced up toward Stella. "She just had knee replacement surgery. Gram used to be a Rockette."

"And I should be practicing my kicks instead of taking it easy. That charity reunion is this summer."

"Yes, but Gram, you don't want to reinjure yourself."

The older Mrs. Perkins aimed an annoyed glance toward her son. "Telling tales, Roger?"

He kissed her cheek. "Only the truth. The physical therapist said you're to be doing only the exercises she prescribed. Your stair obsession is going to land you back in the rehab center."

Charlotte shuddered. "More doctors."

Stella tried to hide a smile, but Owen openly laughed. "Can't complain too much, Gram Gram. Stella's going to be a doctor."

"No, she's right to complain," Stella said. "That's the first thing we learn in med school. How to wake up patients just as they fall asleep. Unnecessary vital checks. Probing questions about the bathroom. Honestly, we make it as annoying as possible so you won't want to stay in the examination room or hospital bed."

Charlotte laughed. "Finally the truth comes out. You'll be welcome here even when I kick out that son and grandson of mine for constantly being on my case. And what a lovely blouse."

Had the older woman not recognized her shirt or was she deadpanning? "Thanks. Had I known it was your birthday, I would have brought you something. Obviously free medical advice is out."

Charlotte shuddered again. "Just you luring my grandson home for the weekend is gift enough," she said loudly and with a wave of her hands. "You can slip me some vodka later," she whispered for Stella's ears alone. She'd definitely deadpanned the shirt bit.

Owen straightened and reached for Stella's hand. "C'mon, I'll introduce you to the rest of the family. You met Bethany already," he said as he drew her toward the airy kitchen. "These are my other sisters, Amelia and Daphne."

Whereas Owen and Bethany favored their mother, Amelia and Daphne both resembled their dad. Dark brown eyes and hair, no hint of a honey tint.

"No offense, but why are you with this guy?" Amelia asked, then kissed her brother's cheek in welcome.

Karen placed her hand on her son's shoulder. "Owen, grab a few more logs for the fire. I can just picture your gram going outside tonight after we leave."

His eyes widened and he glanced down at Stella. "Um—"

His mother gave him a little push. "Go. She'll be just fine."

Now it was Stella's turn for her eyes to widen. She now understood Karen's motivation for Owen's impromptu errand. Separate and interrogate. Without Owen's overwhelming (and protective) presence, Karen could sneak in a few questions. His family assumed they were in a real relationship, and Karen wanted to check her out to see if Stella was good enough for her son.

Should she make a break for it?

Karen patted her hand. "Don't worry. After all, I already know you're going to be a doctor so you'll be able to support our son," she said with a wink.

Bethany snorted. "Yeah, keep him in old trucks and muddy hiking boots."

"So, how'd you two meet?" Daphne asked.

Stella's mouth dried. How had they met? Surrounded

by this loud and loving family, she'd been able to forget this morning. No memory. Handcuffs. Bathtub. Any rational person would be freaking out. Racing around trying to ferret out details. Not holing up inside a beautiful home, eyeing plates of meat and cheese.

Daphne's question sounded casual to the unguarded ear, but all the women directed their full attention on Stella.

"Oh, was it a first-responder thing?" Bethany asked.

Stella grabbed that easy answer and nodded vigorously. But actually, that might not be too far from the truth. Maybe they'd witnessed an accident or spotted someone hurt and both had used their training to help. Maybe they'd been exposed to some kind of drug or breathable agent while they were aiding the victim, it had wiped away their memories, and all last night was some magical mystery they'd never remember.

Once again she longed for her phone so she could check out the headlines.

Owen returned at that moment, carrying an armful of wood. He brought in a blast of cool fall air. He stacked the logs on the hearth, the muscles of his arms stretching and flexing. The man's body was a work of art, the perfect specimen that could be found in one of her anatomy books.

"Oh, yeah, she's got it," Daphne said, and the other sisters laughed.

Stella felt the heat of a flush warm her cheeks. She'd just been caught staring at a man by his sisters. How embarrassing.

Amelia rolled her eyes. "Don't worry about it. In fact, we're used to it. Girls have been drooling over Owen since he was in sixth grade."

Figured. The man had been lethal even as a kid.

"Or friends would try to score an invite to our house or try to spot him after football practice," Bethany told her.

"Football?" Stella asked.

Bethany nodded. "He was the quarterback."

Figured. The quarterback and popular. The exact opposite of her crowd in high school. Or college. She wasn't even in the cool clique in med school.

Yeah, the man was so not her type.

Keep reminding yourself of that. Maybe it will stick.

"But you're the only girl who's actually caught him," Amelia said.

Stella brushed her sweaty palms down her thighs. "Maybe that's because I let him catch me."

Daphne snickered. "I love that you made him chase you. Oh, you're going to fit in perfectly."

Fit in? "Oh, but—"

Amelia nodded. "Yeah, it's nice to see someone not falling at his feet just to please him. I mean, we've tried to take him down a peg or two."

"Or four."

All the sisters laughed.

"C'mon, girls, the rest of this food isn't going to set itself on the table," Karen told them, and Owen's sisters reluctantly returned to the kitchen.

Tormentors. That's what Owen had called them. But hearing it from their end, they'd been doing him a favor. Somewhere in the middle was the truth.

Daphne crossed over to the refrigerator and grabbed a jar of pickles and a squeeze bottle of mayonnaise.

"When he was seven, we convinced him that we'd had another brother, but that our parents were so disappointed in him, they ditched him at a store," Amelia said as she opened a cabinet and pulled down a few serving platters.

Stella's hand flew to her mouth as she followed Daphne to the fridge. "Oh, no."

"After that, he never left our mom's side if we were in a store. It was hilarious."

"But that…that's so mean," Stella said. Why was she feeling sorry for the seven-year-old Owen? The man had come out just fine.

"You never did stuff like that with your brothers and sisters?"

She shook her head. "I'm an only child."

All three sisters looked at her with varying degrees of pity. "Imagine not having a brother," Bethany said.

"Or you guys. Ever," Daphne added.

"Maybe I got off easy," Stella said. "After all, no one made me paranoid my parents were going to leave me in a store." Or shared the Perkinses kids' kind of affection with her. A current of understanding flowed between them. Inside jokes and camaraderie.

Bethany tapped her nose. "True. Ladies, I think the doc has a point."

"And if by *point* you mean we need to help make up for all that she's lost, I'm in," Amelia said with a sly grin.

"Me, too," echoed Daphne. "No offense."

"I'm beginning to understand why Owen's never brought anyone home," Stella grumbled. But his sisters only laughed.

Bethany handed her a stack of bowls. "Just put those on the table."

Stella grabbed the opportunity to escape from the sisters. She took the bowls and crossed to the large dining room table. Her gaze strayed to the gorgeous man who'd brought her here. Owen was hunkered down and talking quietly with his grandma, drawing a smile and a chuckle from the older woman. He added a log to the fire.

"He's always been a firebug," Amelia said.

Nope, no getaway reprieve—his sisters followed her to the table.

"Guess that's why he became a fireman," Stella said, hoping her addition to the conversation would draw attention away from the fact that she'd been checking out their brother's body again.

"But who would have guessed the parachute?" Daphne said with a shrug.

"What?" Stella asked.

"Owen's a smokejumper in Colorado. He didn't tell you that?" Bethany probed, her brows together.

Maybe. Last night.

Karen held her hands over her heart. "The first time I ever saw him at his job, I almost climbed into the plane to drag him out of it. He flies up over a fire in the mountains, then parachutes down."

Stella couldn't fight the shudder that ran down her body.

"You're not a risk-taker?" Amelia asked.

"I've seen plenty of the downside of risk in my job." But honestly, Stella wouldn't even ride a roller coaster. Not that she'd admit that to anyone in Owen's family— that would be a weakness they'd for sure exploit.

"Now, don't take this the wrong way, I mean no offense, Stella, but why are you with my brother?" Daphne asked.

Amelia swatted at her sister's arm. "Daphne."

"What? Obviously he's kept her in the dark about the more dangerous aspects of his job. And let's face it. Since Lily, Owen has gone out of his way to seek any thrill."

Lily?

Daphne returned her attention to Stella. "Do you enjoy

all that extreme stuff, too? The white-water rafting or the BASE jumping or the rock climbing?"

"Uh…no," Stella finally said, crossing her arms across her chest. Great. One of his sisters was sure to spot that tell.

Daphne's gaze narrowed. Stella felt as if she was undergoing an intense visual examination. Then Daphne smiled. "Good. It's time he stopped that crazy-ass stuff."

"Language, Daph," Karen chided.

"What crazy-ass stuff?" Owen asked as he joined them, plopping a slice of cheese into his mouth.

"Language, Owen," Karen said on a heavy sigh.

"Oh, the hang gliding and the cave diving and that wild job of yours."

"Never cave dived, but thanks for the idea."

Karen clapped her hands. "Okay, kids, grab a plate and make a sandwich. We'll eat around the fire so Gram doesn't have to get up."

"I can walk to my own table," Gram called from her seat beside the fire.

Karen's breath came out in a tired hiss. "I knew I should have whispered that. Table it is."

Roger handed Charlotte her cane. The two made slow but steady progress to the ornately carved buffet dining table, now spread with all the fixings for lunch. Stella's stomach grumbled loud enough for Amelia to hear.

"You can get ahead of me in line," she teased.

"Oh, yes. You're our guest, Stella. You come up right behind Gram," Karen directed with a wave of her hands.

"Thanks," she said, aiming for the front of the line, feeling only a tiny bit awkward. But then, when *was* the last time she'd eaten? Her stomach growled again.

"Where do you think you're going?" called Daphne.

Stella whirled around to see Owen on her heels. "Stella's with me. It's only right that I'm with her."

Daphne's lips twisted. "Yeah, sure. Does she need your help to make a sandwich, too? I don't think so. Back of the line, buddy."

Roger shook his head. "No, Owen should be with his guest."

"I'm going to start bringing a guest from now on."

Daphne crossed her arms against her chest. "I'm instituting a one-time guest policy. Next family dinner, you're both at the back."

Owen laughed and Stella shook her head.

"What?" he asked.

"I can't tell what's fighting and what's just teasing. No offense." Had she just said that?

"It's both."

Maybe this meal was a mistake. Owen's sisters were too sharp, and they might already suspect something wasn't gelling between her and their brother. She'd have to be on her guard.

She was supposed to be acting as a buffer between him and his family. Not causing them to ask more questions. Plus their family dynamic was just confusing. Warm and teasing and loud and heated all at the same time.

"Thanks," he whispered into her ear so only she could hear. His warm breath tickled the sensitive skin behind her ear.

"For what?"

"For being here. I'm sure this is awkward as hell for you. Especially after this morning. You may have noticed I haven't been home for a while. You being here has made things, uh…easier."

And right then, a hidden and protected part inside her broke open and gushed all kinds of warm feely things.

Gross.

And damn.

Stella didn't want this. She'd staunchly suppressed all her warm feels for as long as she could remember, and here they were flowing freely without warning in some kind of corny cliché. No. And hell no. "I don't think…"

Then he flashed her such a delicious and tempting smile she forgot what she was going to say. Was it no? Stella leaned toward him and—

"Stop the love talk, you two, and fill your plates. Some of us are hungry."

Over the next hour, Stella received a joyful glimpse of what it might have been like to grow up with such a large family. Overwhelming, yes, but nice, too, with their shared stories and memories and always knowing another sib was there to have your back.

At least it seemed nice until they started in on some of those stories as they were clearing off the table. "Remember that time we convinced Owen his toys were trying to kill him?"

Owen's mother put her hand on her hip. "Is that why I found a garbage bag of your toys stuffed in the garage? I never got a straight answer from any of you."

"Now I don't feel so guilty about putting the hair remover in your shampoo," he said, fighting a smile and failing.

Amelia's mouth dropped and her eyes squinted. "That was you?"

Owen shrugged. "It didn't take off *all* your hair."

"I had to go to the sophomore dance with fuzzy patches."

On second thought, maybe being an only child was the way to go.

Later, in the kitchen, Stella spotted a picture of a little

boy who could only be Owen. Same half smile and hazel eyes. Yeah, the sixth-grade girls hadn't had a chance against his boyish charm. Even as a grown woman, Stella had trouble keeping his alluring appeal in perspective.

Noting Stella's attention on the family pictures, Bethany said, "Everywhere you look you're bombarded by all your previous fashion and hair mistakes."

While she'd first felt on guard around them, after this meal, Stella got the sense Owen's sisters would welcome her into their tight-knit clan with a smile and a glass of sweet tea. That was…if what she had with their brother was real. She'd had no intention of making it anything other than it was right now, of course. Despite her quick reactions to his kiss, and smile, and—oh, hell, everything about the man made her mouth dry. To distract herself, Stella made a show of squinting at the picture of Owen as a young boy.

"What's he wearing?" Stella asked.

"Ahh, that's an invisibility cloak," Bethany said with a chuckle.

"A what?"

"We found this old cape up in the attic. Probably some costume of Gram's she'd forgotten. You get to have the coolest dress-up parties when your grandma was a dancer. Anyway, we told him when he wore it he became invisible."

"And he believed it?"

Even though she was a Perkins and must share their unique flair for inflicting sibling suffering, a guilty look crossed Bethany's face. "We could be pretty convincing." Then the guilt faded and his oldest sister closed her eyes for a moment as if she were trying to contain a laugh. "The places he'd try to go." She opened her eyes.

"When I think about it, we were awfully mean to him. Not that he didn't give it back to us when he was older."

"Who's with him?" Stella asked, pointing to a younger girl dressed in a lopsided princess crown and a boxing glove.

"That was our sister Lily."

Was.

The smile faded from Bethany's face and her voice quieted. "Lily was the youngest. We all adored her, but she and Owen were closest."

"How did she—"

"Cancer." Bethany breathed in deep. "So it was slow. Lots of long stays in the hospital." She tapped a picture with her fingernail of Owen at around twenty. "He shaved his head because Lily had lost all her hair from the chemo. He'd do anything for her. He changed after she died," Bethany said, her voice filled with sadness.

He'd become a hero, a firefighter and a lifesaver. But also a risk-taker. He'd moved away from those closest to him but still clearly missed them.

"It's nice to see my brother happy. With you."

Stella's throat tightened. Guilt. Not an emotion she usually tolerated. Now it twisted inside her stomach. She'd never imagined when she accepted the lunch invitation in the shed that his family would think she and Owen had some kind of long-term relationship. Maybe she could slink out of here. She didn't need answers about last night. Or any more lip-locks with this woman's handsome brother.

Bethany squeezed her hands. "Thank you for bringing him back to us."

With a heavy sigh, Stella straightened her shoulders. In a few short hours she'd be out of his, and their, lives, but Owen had a lifetime sentence with these people. She couldn't leave them assuming she'd been responsible for healing his pain.

Stella shook her head. "He brought himself. It's not my doing. Your brother got here all on his own. He was ready."

Bethany ceded a tight smile and nodded. "I missed him. We all have. You're supposed to lean on your family in times of trouble, but he pushed us away. I understand why. We all reminded him of what he lost when Lily died."

Stella wanted to look anywhere but at Owen's sister. Emotion radiated from Bethany in waves. Sadness. Love. Loss and regret. This, *this* was why Stella was so much better suited for emergency medicine. Patients came in and out. Tragedy and joy and relief came in quick, short bursts. Not long surges of draining emotion. Moments like this threatened her detachment. Emotions didn't belong in medicine. They clouded judgment and adversely affected patient care.

She met Bethany's gaze, feeling inept and terrified she was about to bungle this hardcore. Stella frantically searched for the right words to say, one nugget of wisdom that would give comfort and ease this woman's pain. But nothing came. Would her bedside manner ever improve?

Owen's sister wiped her cheek with the back of her hand. "Wow, I had no idea that was going to come out today." Bethany gripped Stella's shoulder and gave her a light squeeze. "Thanks. I really needed that. I'd better go put on a pot of coffee."

"You're welcome," she muttered to Bethany's retreating back, a little stunned.

Stella pushed a few stray strands of her hair out of her eyes and searched the room, searching for an escape route. And then her gaze smacked into Owen's, and the breath left her body in a whoosh. Owen. That's what, or in this case, *who*, she'd been searching for a moment ago. And she hadn't even realized it. Her heartbeat kicked up a notch.

An hour ago she'd wanted nothing more than to get out of the handcuffs and never see this guy again. And now…what did she want?

In a few long strides he was at her side. "You okay?" he asked close to her ear, the rich timbre of his voice sending erotic quivers down her neck to pool in the small of her back.

She nodded. How many ranges of emotion was a person supposed to have slam into her in the course of thirty seconds? She'd gone from guilt to worry to uncertainty and then taken a one-eighty to relief and desire.

"Things looked intense with you and my sister."

She nodded. "They've really missed you. How long since you've been home?"

"Three years," he admitted, his voice tight.

Her fingers curled around his forearm and his muscles bunched beneath her fingertips. "Owen, they think that I'm responsible for this miraculous change in you, and I'm the reason you came back for your grandmother's party. I made sure Bethany understood it was all you."

He shifted his weight from his left leg to his right and then back again. "Yeah, uh…thanks."

Stella glanced over at the rest of Owen's family. They'd migrated to the overstuffed furniture in front of the roaring fireplace, chatting happily and stealing peeks in Stella and Owen's direction every now and then.

"I had no idea they'd be shipping us so hard."

Owen rubbed the back of his neck. "No, that caught me off guard, too. Sometime in the past three years, my parents have moved into major grandparent mode. Too bad none of us are even close to a real relationship."

"Maybe if they hadn't caught you kissing me they wouldn't have gotten the wrong idea."

The green in his hazel eyes turned deep and seductive. "I remember it as you kissing me last. Looking at my mouth. Like you are now."

The corners of her lips tugged until she knew she had to be grinning like an idiot. "No, you definitely kissed me last."

He grinned back at her and tingles shot up and down her spine. "What are you going to do when I never show up here again?" she forced herself to ask. Because she definitely needed cold, hard reality to battle the tingles and sexy smiles and hazel eyes that made a woman want to spend all day rolling between the sheets.

"I'll tell them you broke up with me. Don't worry, they'll have no problem buying that excuse."

And before they could share a moment or his lips could distract her, he changed the subject. Thankfully. "So they're going to want to do coffee, sit and talk more."

"But before they offer, I should make a break for it," she suggested.

His lips pressed together and his gaze fell away. "Something like that."

Owen wheeled around and away from her, but she reached for him. He flinched beneath her fingertips. She asked, "That's the plan, right?"

Her breath caught in her chest. Did she want another plan? More time with this man?

He flashed her an easy smile and gave her a wink. "Of course."

With slow footsteps, Stella followed Owen to the seating area where the rest of his family sat quietly (for them) and talked. Twice she almost stopped him, a sinking sensation delving deeper through her with each step she took. Something had just happened a moment ago between them. Something she was too slow or too closed off to pick up on until the moment had passed.

She glanced toward Owen, who smiled and chuckled at something his dad said. With a delightful dimple in his cheek and crinkles at his eyes from humor, Owen was completely tension-free.

Nope, she'd imagined the moment. Too much studying and not enough sex. Her body had ended that state last night, but her mind hadn't caught up to reality, which was why she projected half a dozen emotions and responses on the sexy-as-hell firefighter across from her. Stella wandered over to the fireplace to warm her now very chilled hands. Karen patted the empty spot beside her, and Stella sat down awkwardly, her shoulders stiff.

"I hope you didn't feel left out with all our stories."

Stella twisted on the cushion. "Oh, no. I had a great time. Scared if I ever get on the bad side of any of your children, but it was fun."

"I think you're a woman who can hold her own. Your family much different?"

There was no teasing at her family's table. Only strict boundaries and respect for others' personal space. "Oh, very. My parents never missed an opportunity for a teachable moment. Meals were more like quizzes and test prep."

"Did I hear you were an only child?" Daphne asked. "What were you doing if you weren't planning your next attack on your brother or sister?"

"I read a lot. I liked to explore." She angled her head toward the large bay window. "The gardens here are beautiful."

Karen smiled. "Oh, that's all Charlotte. She traveled the world as a dancer, but when she decided to settle down with Roger's father, she was determined to bring the world here for her children to share."

Stella nodded. "I spotted the Greek and Mediterranean influences."

"You're going to be Charlotte's favorite person around here. She'd love nothing better than to show you around and tell you about her favorite plants or features. I think that's where Owen gets his love of the outdoors. Although he prefers the more rugged wilderness over our tame little garden. Once she's up and walking around more, Charlotte wants to add a meditation area like we spotted at the Japanese Garden in the Fort Worth Botanic Garden. She's had her eye on a few cherry trees at the nursery. Charlotte, why don't you tell Stella of your plans? You know much more about it than I do."

They both swiveled on the couch so they could talk with the older woman.

Charlotte nodded slowly, with her head tilted at an odd angle. "Yes, I..."

"Charlotte, are you okay?"

The older woman's gaze seemed unfocused, and she opened and closed her mouth several times.

Stella slid off the couch and kneeled in front of Charlotte, noting the pallor of her skin and how the older woman tried to rub at her temples.

"Mrs. Perkins, it appears you're in distress. Do I have your permission to examine you?" Stella asked, her voice firm.

"Of course you have permission," Roger said.

"She's trying to keep Gram alert, Dad." Owen crouched beside her.

Charlotte closed her eyes briefly, and Stella gently

took the older woman's wrist in her hand, feeling for the radial pulse. A fluttery, irregular beat thumped beneath her fingertips.

She met Owen's concerned gaze. "I think she's in A-fib. Could be a stroke."

The teasing, sexy near-stranger disappeared, replaced by the professional first responder. "Dad, call 911. Mom, get all Gram Gram's medicines, everything she's taking, even if it's not on a regular basis, and put them in a bag."

"Should we get her something? A glass of water?" Bethany asked.

"Shouldn't you be giving her CPR or something?" Daphne said, her voice breaking.

Stella shook her head. "No, she's breathing just fine." She smiled at Mrs. Perkins. "Right now we're all going to keep her calm until the ambulance arrives."

"Ambulance. Oh, no, Gram—"

Stella cleared her throat to get their attention. "Daphne, why don't you and Bethany pack a nightgown for your grandmother. I'm sure she'd prefer to sleep in her own clothes instead of a scratchy hospital gown."

The two sisters raced for the stairs and the room instantly quieted.

After a few minutes they heard sirens blaring in the distance, announcing help was close.

Owen turned toward his remaining sister, who stood in the corner, wringing her hands. "Amelia, open the front door for the EMTs."

With a nod, she rushed toward the door.

A few minutes later, the great room was filled with first responders, their equipment and a stretcher.

"Maybe you should ride with her to the hospital, Stella," Roger suggested, his face lined with worry.

But Stella shook her head. "The EMTs will take great

care of her, and I'm a stranger to her. You go. She'll want to be with family."

After the ambulance left, Karen and Owen's sisters took the family car along with a suitcase of Charlotte's belongings. Stella and Owen raced to his truck. They drove in tense silence to the hospital and were ushered into the ER waiting area when they arrived.

Karen talked in quiet voices with her daughters while Roger sat in a corner, his hands in fists. Owen paced. Stella just stood awkwardly to the side, feeling like an intruder in what should have been a private family moment.

As much time as she'd spent in emergency rooms, Stella had never been on this side of the door. Oh, she'd fetched family members to ask health histories or to escort them to their sick relatives, but Stella had never had to wait anxiously for news. Seeing Roger's stony expression and Owen's leashed anger and his sisters' quiet strength gave her a whole different perspective as a future doctor.

After thirty minutes, a resident in rumpled scrubs came out from the examination area. The entire Perkins clan rushed to surround her, their shoes squeaking on the vinyl floor.

"It wasn't a stroke," the resident assured them.

Roger's shoulders sagged in relief, and then he wrapped his arms around his wife while his daughters hugged one another.

Only Owen wasn't happy. "What was it?"

The resident consulted the chart for a moment, then addressed the family. "Mrs. Perkins had a bad reaction to her medications. With the confusion and the slurring of speech, it could have easily been interpreted as a stroke. Had it been, your quick action could have saved her from most if not all permanent damage."

Karen slipped out from under her husband's arm. The older woman reached for Stella's hand, gave her a squeeze and drew her into the comforting circle of the family. "Thanks to Stella."

The resident nodded and directed her attention to Stella. "I understand you have some medical training."

"I start my next round of clinicals after fall breakfast."

"Oh, yeah? Never skip breakfast. Might be the only meal you have all day. And night."

"Good to know." Maybe she should offer to run to the snack bar or a vending machine.

The resident returned her attention to Roger. "Your mother's comfortable and on an IV right now. We're waiting for a bed upstairs. I'd like her to stay overnight. There were a lot of meds in that bag. Good thinking on the part of whoever brought that in with her. Has there been a change in her prescriptions recently?"

Karen shook her head. "She had knee surgery, but it's been several weeks."

"Sometimes it can take a while for compounds to build up in the system or for a body to react. For the time being I only want Mrs. Perkins on her blood pressure and heart meds." The resident held up a finger. "And from now on, she needs to see one doctor, a primary, who oversees all her medications and coordinates between her specialists."

"When can we see her?" Owen asked.

"Now, but let's keep it to one person at a time. Once she's moved upstairs she will be allowed multiple visitors."

Roger nodded. "I'd like to see my mother."

"Follow me."

Roger kissed his wife's cheek and shadowed the resident down the hall and into the emergency room. Karen turned toward her daughters. "Okay, girls, let's find a decent cup of coffee."

Owen scrubbed a hand down the back of his neck. "I've got to get out of here."

Stella raced to catch up with him. The man weaved around several different hallways until finding a courtyard. She was winded by the time she caught up with him, and resolved—again—to work on her cardio.

"Owen," she called.

He blanched when he spotted her. "Hell, I'm sorry, I—"

"Hey, it's okay. I understand."

He squeezed his eyes shut. "I hate hospitals. The stale coffee and the long hallways and the constant beeping. Just the smell of the cleaner that permeates every single space makes my stomach clench. How can you stand it?"

Stella shrugged. "Been following one or both of my parents through the halls of a hospital for as long as I can remember. Guess I'm just used to it." She paused a moment and took a breath. "It's why you left, isn't it? Too much time in a place like this."

He squinted against the weak fall sunlight, then slid his sunglasses in place. "How'd you guess?"

"You're a close family. It would take something big for you to want to leave them."

"That's something they never understood. I didn't want to leave them. I just needed someplace... Hell, I don't know how to describe it, but I needed to be anywhere that wasn't Dallas."

"And you chose someplace completely different, with tall Colorado pines and the mountains in the distance."

He slumped on one of the metal benches in the courtyard. "Thought you said your bedside manner sucked. You were pretty good with my whole family. Got my sisters doing something other than panicking and gave my dad a job to do."

"That's only because I knew them. I mean..." She sagged right beside him on the bench. The cold of the metal seeped into her skin through her clothes. She liked Owen's family, had grown to care about them in the short time she'd spent with them. She couldn't have been emotionless with them if she'd tried.

Her breath hitched in her chest. She couldn't have been emotionless with them and she *hadn't* tried. Stella had not only functioned as a doctor but also managed to steer that big, loud family into a productive unit *because* she'd cared. She'd connected with Bethany earlier, too, as they'd talked about Lily. All she'd done was listen.

The key to her unique brand of healing couldn't be that easy. Or that hard. To allow even a trickle of emotion into her work violated everything her parents had always cautioned and advised.

Stella stood, her abrupt movement kicking up a few pebbles at her feet. "I need to borrow your phone."

"Sure, of course. Damn, Stella, with all that's been going on, I forgot you wanted to call your roommate. Good thing I charged it over lunch." Owen dug into his pocket and wrangled out his phone.

She nodded. "It's okay. I won't be long."

After a few rings, Janey answered. "Thought you would be home by now. Did your test run late?" her friend asked.

"Test?" Stella's heart began to pound.

"Yeah, you called last night to tell me you were going to volunteer for one of those drug trials."

Although really hazy a vague memory clicked into place like tumblers on a lock safe. Her hands began to tremble and she gripped Owen's phone tighter. No one had drugged them last night with intent to rob them or do them harm. She'd volunteered to be drugged. Though experimental medication didn't explain how she'd ended up handcuffed and naked in a bathtub—wait, scratch that. Yes, actually, it did. One look at Mr. Not For Her and she would have instantly wanted Owen. Add close proximity and maybe a little drug loopiness and, yeah, she'd hand-cuff herself to the man.

A few more tidbits of information and she could find her car and her phone. "Did I say which company I vol-unteered with last night?"

"Uh, Pharma something."

"That's helpful," she grumbled. "Half the developers probably have Pharma in their name."

"Sorry, Stella. I—"

"No, I'm sorry," she said. "I don't think I got a lot of sleep last night." As evidenced by the tenderness of some of her more intimate muscles. "I'm just cranky. My car's not in the parking lot, by any chance?"

Please be there. Please be there.

"Nope. I don't see it."

Stella's shoulders slumped. Well, she couldn't expect Janey to solve every mystery. But she could figure it all out with a bit of reason. If her car wasn't at her apartment and it wasn't at the hotel, the most likely place would be the testing facility. "I'll be home in a bit. Oh, wait, will you be home?"

"Yeah, why?"

"I might have lost my keys last night."

"You?" Janey asked, her voice teasing. "That doesn't sound like something the most responsible person in the world would do."

"Yeah. You know what else isn't something I would do? I ended my man-drought, too. I'll be home in a bit."

Janey gasped. "Wait. Stella, you—"

Stella couldn't stop a broad smile from crossing her face. "Sorry, gotta go." She pressed the End button, enjoying the tiny bit of joy that shot through her from her teasing torment. Whoa. The Perkins clan was rubbing off on her.

She found Owen gazing down at a row of ants on the ground as they moved from underneath a rock to a pile of leaves and back again. He'd escaped to the rugged and wild West to heal after his sister's death. Their hotel room had looked out over a gorgeous courtyard. The man enjoyed nature. But it was more than that. A refuge. Stella decided to hang back and allow him to be alone with his thoughts.

But he glanced up just as she took a step away. Owen straightened, dusted his hands off his jeans and smiled at her. "All done?"

She nodded, because what else could she do? This gorgeous man, who fought fires for a living and parachuted into places most everyone else would run screaming from, smiled at her like she was the best thing he'd seen. Her heart went all fluttery and she swallowed, because he was the best thing she'd seen, too.

Of course she knew all about the heady combination of adrenaline and dopamine and serotonin that made rational human beings risk everything for more of the love drugs. Her mind didn't remember the rush she must have shared with this man, but her body sure did. Or maybe her body didn't remember, either, but anticipated something fiery with him, because if (when?) they got together beneath the sheets, the sex between them would be explosive.

His phone buzzed in her hand, and she glanced down to see he'd gotten a text. "For you," she said and handed it over to him. His fingers were rough and calloused in places, and his light grazing touch sent a shaft of sensation down her arm.

Owen punched in the code for his phone. His head fell back after he read the text, his face seeking the sun. Her shoulders tensed. "News?" she asked.

He looked at her. "The best. Gram's in a room and she's responding to the saline flush. She's sleepy but wants us to visit her tomorrow. We're also to save her at least one piece of the chocolate cake."

Stella laughed. "That's great. My roommate gave me some good news, too. Or at least some info that's a relief. We weren't drugged last night. I volunteered for some kind of overnight drug trial. I must have met you there."

Comprehension flooded his gaze, and he nodded. "That makes sense. Ever since Lily…"

He didn't have to finish his sentence. Ever since his sister's death, Owen must have volunteered to be a human guinea pig so others might not have to suffer or die like Lily. If Stella didn't already have a serious case of want for this man, she would now.

"So, I, uh—" she began.

"Well, if you're—" He stopped. "You first."

"I was going to ask if you'd drop me off at my apartment. You probably want to get back to your family."

"What about finding your car, and your purse?"

"I'm sure my car is at the testing lab. I must have, uh, left with you." Heat flooded her cheeks at the admission she'd wanted this man so badly she hadn't even bothered to secure her vehicle.

"We've got the handcuffs off. We might as well stop off at the hotel first for your purse."

Stella had never been one to argue with logic, but she really wanted to at the moment. Which, yeah, was pretty childish, but the prospect of returning to the scene of their lovemaking created a ton of flutters in her stomach.

Was she afraid she couldn't resist him? Absolutely. No way could she battle against her desire for him any longer. All afternoon she'd teetered on the edge of admitting just how much she wanted him. The long glances. The teasing kisses. It had been one long afternoon of foreplay. Heightened by the emotional danger and turmoil of waking up naked with a stranger, finding those notes, the knock at the door and finally his grandmother's health scare.

But that was exactly the reason why they had to stick to the plan. Desire and emotion would wreck her entire life plan. So they'd go to the hotel, grab her purse and say goodbye. A simple, rational plan. What could go wrong?

8

THE SUITED ATTENDANT at the amazing hand-carved check-in desk of the Market Gardens eyed their clothes with a raise of the eyebrow. Owen was wearing the same clothes he'd been wearing yesterday, and she was wearing a grandma blouse.

"Perkins. There was supposed to be an item left for me at the front desk," Owen said, his voice not unfriendly but curt. In fact, his entire demeanor had been abrupt since he'd slid in beside her on the quilt-covered bench of the truck. He'd spoken little as he drove through the Dallas streets, his fingers drumming random patterns on the steering wheel.

The attendant typed something on the discreetly hidden keypad. "Yes, housekeeping recovered the purse and returned it to your room."

"I checked out this morning. It was supposed to have been left for us here."

The clerk typed in a few more words, but his brow furrowed at whatever message must have popped up on his screen. "I'm sorry for any confusion. We have you checking out tomorrow at noon. I'm more than happy to cancel your reservation, but then you'll have to wait for security to enter the room on your behalf to retrieve the purse again."

"How long would that take?" Stella asked, feeling cranky and restless and ready to get out of here.

"It would be down here within the hour."

"You said my reservation is still good?" Owen asked.

"Yes."

"So that means my key card will work, yes?"

The desk clerk nodded.

"Then we'll key in, grab the purse and drop off the card on the way out the door," Owen told him.

But the man behind the desk was already shaking his head.

Owen scrubbed a hand down his face. "Look, it's been a hell of a day for us."

"Five minutes," Stella added.

The desk clerk eyed the clock in a lavish gilt frame. "Cancellation of a stay is required by six. If you're up and down by that time, fine. Otherwise I'll have to charge you for the extra night."

Owen grabbed her hand. "Done." And they raced for the elevator along the hardwood floors. She resisted the urge to run her fingers through the water of the two-tiered fountain. They had seven minutes.

Mirrors edged the walls of the elevator and she was surrounded by images of Owen as the doors closed. She sucked in a breath and forced herself to think of rational things. "I keep hoping something will trigger my memory of last night," she said.

He leaned his head against the glass, but his gaze found hers. "I'd give anything to remember."

The primal part of her, the one she kept hidden and tightly leashed at all times, responded to the huskiness of his voice in the most carnal of ways. Her lips parted, and a shiver ran between her shoulder blades. His gaze drifted to her mouth and then lower when her nipples hardened. From not even a touch. Just a look.

"Do you remember this elevator from last night?" she asked, because the sensations he stirred were just too powerful. Too sensual. Her body had to be responding to the memory of his embrace. His heated caresses. The carnal touch of his breath on her skin.

"No, but I know what I would have done."

Her breath hitched. Her racing thoughts suddenly stalled. Even her heart seemed to stop beating for a moment. Because this was *it*—the single tick of time that could alter everything between them.

But, as Stella had learned over the past twenty-four hours, the detached approach wasn't always the best one. Maybe her drug-induced self had had the right idea.

"What would you have done?" Stella asked, knowing what she was inviting.

He whirled her around so that she was facing the mirror, her back pressed alongside his chest and the hard ridge of his cock nestled against her ass. Their gazes met in the mirror, and she watched as he twined his fingers through hers and lifted her arm. He bent her arm at the elbow, and she cupped the back of his head. Then he brushed down her skin with the backs of his fingers, tingles jetting from wherever he touched.

"This," he whispered against her neck, then drew his tongue up the column of her throat. She shivered.

His hand stroked down her body, stopping to span her hips, then rising again to cover her breasts. Her nipples hardened to agonizing points of pleasure to meet his touch. With a groan, he caressed her breasts. Her eyes closed, the sensation of it too much.

The elevator dinged and the doors slowly slid open.

Owen left her with a gentle kiss right below her ear. She followed him out and the doors closed behind her. The lighting was more discreet in the hallway, nothing harsh or distracting to make a person rethink what they were doing.

Like entering a hotel room with a stranger, as you did the night before.

The thick carpet masked her footsteps, and when Owen reached the door to their hotel room, he turned slowly, as if he almost expected she wouldn't be there.

That sexy half smile of his was her reward, and he reached for the leather holder containing the key card. His hand paused over the swiper. "You can stay out here," he told her. "I'll go in, grab your purse and then take you home."

"Is that what you want?"

"Hell no."

She lifted his chin with her finger and then looped her arms behind his neck. "Me, either."

Stella raised her lips, and he wrapped his arms around her back and drew her flush against the hardness of his chest with a groan. Oh, what that groan did to her.

"Open the door, Owen," she whispered against his lips.

His arm dropped, and she smiled as he swiped the card too fast for the light to flash red. "Damn." He swiped again and she sighed in relief when the lock flashed green and snicked open.

She was in his arms and up against the wall before the door even closed. His mouth was on hers and his tongue slid inside in one breath-stealing kiss. Stella palmed his biceps and back, feeling the strength in his coiled muscles. Balancing on one foot, Stella hooked her leg around his hips, positioning his cock at the cleft between her legs. She breathed in his scent on a moan, reveled in the heightened heat of his body. "Mmmmm."

Owen jutted his hips into hers, and she moaned again at the exquisite pleasure of the thrust against her clit. "I so wish I could remember last night."

He dropped a kiss on the corner of her mouth. "There's nothing that says we can't."

"What do you mean?"

"Do you remember this?" he asked and rubbed her bottom lip gently with the calloused pad of his thumb.

She shook her head. "But do it again."

"How about this?" He ran his tongue along her bottom lip instead.

She darted out her tongue to touch his, but he ducked away from her. "I gotta make a call," he said.

"Now?" She slumped against the wall, feeling confused and a tiny bit vulnerable.

He lifted the receiver and pushed only one button. His dark hazel eyes never left hers. "We're keeping the room."

Her purse waited for her on the intimate dining table, but Stella couldn't have cared less. Right now, she planned to finally get naked in bed with this unbelievable man.

"Damn you're the sexiest woman I've ever seen. What is it about you?" he asked after he dropped the phone into the cradle and crossed to where she leaned against the wall.

"It's nature's little trick to make sure we keep going."

"Mmm, that makes sense. But why, when we all were sitting around the table at lunch, could I only think of kissing you?"

Stella drew a lazy path down his chest with her finger. "It's your testosterone. You're aroused and when you kiss me, you pass that testosterone on to me, making me more aroused, too."

"Like this?" he asked, and lowered his lips to hers. She lifted her open mouth and her tongue twined with his. It was the kind of intense kiss that slowed time and dragged want and need from every hidden place. Their shared lip-lock left her breathless and hungry.

"Do you remember kissing me like this last night?"

She shook her head. "But I'm game to figure out what we don't remember. You have a hundred more nerve endings in your lips." She lifted her mouth and rubbed her mouth against his. "Plus kisses elevate your heart rate and get the blood flowing so it's easier to reach orgasm."

He chuckled deep in his throat and her body reacted with a shiver. "This science talk of yours, Doc, is kind of sexy. Never would have thought it." He rubbed his lips against hers. "Now tell me why I want to look into your eyes. I've never seen such amazing brown eyes."

Owen locked his gaze with her own and Stella had to remind herself to breathe. "Survival. Most of our communication is done without words." Stella glanced toward the floor. "If I don't meet your gaze, maybe I have something to hide, and you'll know not to trust me." Then she stared into his eyes. "But if I meet your gaze, you can see how much I want your mouth on mine and your hands on my body. It's a chemical. Phenylethylamine."

Owen cupped her breasts. His thumbs stroked her nipples through her shirt.

"What's the scientific reason I get so much pleasure from stroking your breasts? Why do I ache to hear your breath catch—yes, just like that—when my touch pleases you?"

Stella shook her head. "I don't remember anymore. Just don't stop."

His head swooped down and she lifted on her toes and met his kiss. He palmed her breasts until her nipples turned into tight points that rubbed inside the soft fabric of her bra. She had to get out of her clothes.

Stella flattened her palms against his chest and shoved him back. Then she reached for the buttons of her blouse. His heavy-lidded gaze lowered, watching as she worked her way down her shirt. "Do you remember this from last night?" she asked.

He shook his head. "No, I probably would have wanted to take that flimsy thing off you myself."

"Do you want me to stop?" she teased.

"Hell, no. I could watch this show all night."

"Good, because I plan to keep you occupied for the rest of the evening."

"We should continue. In the interest of science."

Her shirt dropped at her feet. "In the interest of science." She hooked her finger around the strap of her bra, tugging down the left then the right. Next Stella reached for the hooks, and in a moment her bra fell at her feet silently.

Her nipples puckered at the change in air temperature and from the heavy weight of Owen's gaze. "Better than I could have imagined." He toyed with her nipple, watching it react to his touch. "I'm kind of glad I don't remember last night."

"Why?"

"Because now I get to have two first times with you." Owen closed his eyes and began to chuckle.

"What?" she asked.

"That might be the corniest thing I've ever said. In my life."

She grabbed his hands and placed them on her breasts. "Maybe I won't remember tonight, either."

He began to fondle and stroke her breasts. "Oh, you'll remember," he promised.

Stella gripped the bottom of his shirt and pulled it from his jeans. Once it was over his head, she finally got to revel in the work of art that was Owen's chest. Chiseled from hard work and roped with muscle. A scar slashed across his ribcage and she traced the marred skin.

"You were burned?" she asked, knowing the telltale signs.

"It happens. I was being stupid." He shrugged.

There was more to the story, but he wasn't ready to talk about it. That was okay. Owen was allowed his secrets. It wasn't as if she needed to solve all the mysteries of a man she wouldn't be seeing after this weekend.

Stella dropped to her knees and traced the puckered skin with her tongue.

"Oh, so worth it," he hissed through clenched teeth.

"You know what else I can take care of while I'm down here?"

"My every fantasy?"

"If by *fantasy* you mean unbuckling your belt, then yes."

She slid the leather through the buckle and unbuttoned his jeans. He groaned as she stood. "Ahh, you were thinking something else?"

"Have to admit I was hoping. You're a tease, woman," he said, his smile tender. He gripped her by the hips, his cock hard and ready. Heat flooded between her legs. He dragged his lips along her collarbone. "I really wanted to take this slow and build you up, but darlin', I want you so bad." She heard a hint of Texan in his voice and thrilled at the need lacing his words.

"You can go slow later. I'm already built up."

"Damn, I left my duffel bag in the truck. My protection is in there."

Being a medical volunteer meant Owen had a clean bill of health, but she always carried protection even when she never planned on getting lucky. "I should have something for us to use in my purse."

The two of them rushed toward the tiny dinette. She snapped her purse open and out fell her car keys. That was one concern resolved. She felt around inside her bag until she found not only her phone but also several square packages. Stella grabbed them all.

She crossed toward the bedroom, but stopped when she noticed Owen hadn't followed. "Change your mind?" she asked.

"Do you remember the bed from last night?"

She shook her head. "Not remembering hasn't stopped us yet."

"What I do remember was waking up in the bathtub with the most gorgeous woman I've ever met."

"So let's hop in and see if it triggers anything."

They dashed to the bathroom hand in hand, but Stella stopped at the threshold. "Wow. Just wow. When you pick a hotel, you know how to pick one."

"This hotel certainly has a thing for mirrors." Reflective glass stretched from the floor to the ceiling of the bathroom. Blue candles the color of Texas bluebonnets lined the tub along with an assortment of bath gels and organic soap. Fluffy towels were stacked in a basket at the foot of the tub, and with a push of a button, a fire would roar to life in the fireplace.

"Why have a fireplace in a bathroom?" he asked.

"So I won't be cold when I do this," she said, and slid her leggings down to her ankles. She kicked them, along with her shoes, to the side.

"Love fireplaces in bathrooms."

Stella stood before him in nothing but her favorite pair of black panties made of delicate scalloped lace, surrounded by dozens of images of her nearly naked self. "You have too many clothes on," she instructed.

She reached for the spigot to adjust the temperature and fill the tub. Something flirty and sensual awakened inside her when she heard his jeans hit the tiled floor. Then Owen was behind her, his cock against her leg. Their gazes met in the mirrored wall.

"Watch me touch you." He caressed and stroked her breasts, over her ribcage and down her stomach. Her knees weakened when she both saw and felt his fingers steal beneath the fabric of her panties. "Watch me," he urged when her eyes fluttered.

He grazed the tip of her clit and she moaned. "Do you remember this from last night?" he asked, his voice raw and husky.

She shook her head. "All I care about is now."

Owen stroked the sensitive bud of nerves again while his other hand cupped her breast, steadying her to his chest. His fingers searched lower. "You're so wet." He slid his hand from her clit to where she craved his body over and over, cupping her in slow, agonizing caresses.

Just when she thought she would come from watching him touch her alone, he stopped. He slipped his hand out from her panties and hooked his thumbs around the narrow straps of black lace, gliding the fabric down her legs.

He tapped her thighs, urging them apart. Cool air brushed along her newly exposed skin, tickling her already throbbing clit. He cupped between her legs again and then slipped a finger inside her. Her knees did buckle then, but he took her weight, kissing her temple. He glided another finger inside her and stroked her inside and out.

"Are you ready for me, Stella?"

She wanted to shout *yes, a thousand times, yes*, but managed to sigh out only one yes.

He led her to the large soaker tub, which was only partially full. She stepped into the water. It was a little cool against her heated skin, but she had the warmth from the fire on one side and the heat of Owen's solid body on the other. He poured bath gel into his hand and then began to smooth it on her skin in gentle little circles.

A light honeysuckle scent filled her nose. She held out her hands to him, and Owen squeezed gel onto her palms. Then she began to rub and work the gel into his chest. She'd never realized how erotic it would be to touch a man like this. They squeezed out more, until every part of them was slick with the gel and bubbles floated in the air. But she was done with just touching him. She needed him inside her.

Stella gripped him by the shoulders and pushed him against the back of the tub. After drying her hands on a towel, she reached for the condom wrapper and ripped it apart with her teeth. Owen lifted his hips from the shallow water and she slid the condom in place, loving the strength of his hard penis. She straddled him then, teased herself and him for a moment, and then sank down.

"Stella. How could I have forgotten this? You feel amazing. You are amazing."

She silenced him with her lips, loving the way her slick breasts slid along his chest as his tongue plunged past her lips. Stella moved along the shaft of his cock until she found a rhythm that forced moans from both of them. His hands settled along her ass and helped to guide her up and down.

Pleasure rocked through her core and her muscles began to clamp around him. Her movements grew more frantic as she tried to reach the peak. She felt the unexpected glide of his fingers between them. He stroked at her clit, demanding a response from her. "Don't stop, Owen."

He bucked his hips, driving his cock deeper and she went over the edge into ultimate pleasure. He rocked inside her, once, twice and then he groaned his satisfaction as he held her tight against his chest.

After a few moments their breathing steadied and the hiss and crackle of the fire and the drip of water from the faucet replaced the sounds of his guttural moans and her ecstatic sighs. He tucked her head against the crook of his neck as the water cooled around them. "That, I will never forget."

SOFT SHAFTS OF light woke Owen the next morning. He rolled over in the bed to bury his nose in Stella's hair. The scent of her drove him crazy. A good kind of crazy. But his hand found only cold, empty sheets. He sat up, rubbing his eyes.

"Stella?" he called.

No answer.

He flung the sheets back and knocked on the bathroom door. The door creaked open behind his knuckles, but the light was off and no one was inside. The door between the bedroom and the living area remained closed. Maybe she'd needed some coffee and didn't want to wake him. He imagined the lovely doc sitting on the couch wrapped in nothing but a blanket. Or better yet, completely naked. Owen circled to the living area and twisted the knob, but that room was empty, too.

His gaze swung to the tiny table where she'd left her purse the night before. Gone. So were her shirt and sexy little red bra they'd dropped next to the front door. He knew without looking that her pants and shoes had vanished along with the woman who'd rocked his night. Stella had ditched him.

After retrieving his duffel bag from the truck, Owen hit the shower. Alone. Not what he'd planned for this morning. Last night, Stella had wrapped herself around his body and used his chest for a pillow, her hand just inches from his cock. As sleep finally took over his exhausted body, he'd imagined leading Stella into the shower in the morning and figuring out more ways to get clean. And dirty.

He slammed the spigot over to cold. The hard needles of the frigid water kicked his sorry ass. So she'd snuck out this morning. She'd saved them both an awkward goodbye. It wasn't like anything more than great sex and a few laughs was going to come out of this weekend. His future was in Colorado. His past would stay in Texas.

She'd done them both a favor.

Owen reminded himself of that favor as he drove back to the hospital, her light berry perfume still haunting the truck. And he reminded himself again of that damn favor as he passed by the courtyard where he'd held Stella in his arms and she'd kissed him like she couldn't get enough of him.

The door to Gram's room stood slightly ajar, and he maneuvered between the cramped space of the door and the frame in case the door creaked when he opened it and awakened her. Then he stopped, because there, sitting in a pool of lamplight, sat Stella. She'd changed her clothes and her dark, curly hair was still damp from a shower, but Owen had never seen anything better.

Something must have alerted her to his presence because she stiffened and glanced up at the door. Her lips parted in a nervous smile, and he found himself smiling back. Probably like an idiot.

"Hey," she whispered.

"Hi." He crossed the room toward her, more relieved than he'd ever believed possible at discovering her in this room. "I thought you'd left."

She lifted a brow. "And did that bother you?"

He rubbed the back of his neck. "More than I care to admit."

But the warm and sexy smile she flashed him made his confession worth it. "Good to hear."

"Why'd you leave?"

"I wanted to catch morning rounds to speak to Charlotte's doctor. Your grandma's doing great. She'll get to leave tonight. In the morning at the latest."

"No, I mean, why'd you leave?" Why did he sound like a whiny moron with this woman?

She lifted a brow. "I did kiss you. You didn't even budge. I figured you needed your sleep."

He crouched down in front of her chair. "Yeah, to recuperate," he whispered. "I'm all rested now."

"Did you not get my note?"

"You left a note?" Yeah, that would have saved him some agony.

Her eyes widened. "Apparently we're really bad at leaving notes."

He scratched at his chin. "You know, if you tried that morning kiss thing again now, you'd get a better reaction."

"Oh, would you two get out of here and let an old lady get some sleep?"

Owen straightened. "Gram." He leaned over the bed to kiss her temple. "How are you feeling this morning?"

"Like someone ran me over with a truck, and when that didn't work, they ran me over with a tractor."

"So just like new?" he asked, his voice teasing.

STELLA WATCHED THE pair talk quietly in the hospital room until his grandmother's eyelids began to drift shut.

Stella placed her arm on his bicep. "We shouldn't wear her out. I'm sure a whole room full of Perkinses will be showing up any minute."

Charlotte's unsteady hand reached for Stella. She leaned in toward the other woman. "I'm older than dirt and I've traveled the world and met a lot of different folks. One thing I've learned is that sometimes people come into your life exactly when you need them. That's you."

The back of Stella's throat began to tighten, and she felt her objectivity slipping. "I'm just glad I was there to be able to help you when I could."

"I was talking about Owen," she whispered. "You came into his life just when he needed you."

"You wouldn't fake being sick just to be a match-maker, would you?" she teased.

A slow smile spread across Charlotte's lips.

"Okay, ladies, break it up." Owen stood and squeezed his grandmother's hands. "You know how to make a birthday memorable."

"Always make an entrance..."

"Always leave them wanting more," he finished, obviously a fond ritual between the two.

Owen matched his stride to Stella's shorter one as he walked beside her down the hall. "How'd you get back home?" he asked.

"I took a taxi. Janey was right. My car wasn't there." Had he been disappointed?

"Our last mystery. Did you eat breakfast?"

She shook her head. "I can just grab something at my apartment."

"You trying to ditch me now?"

She stopped to face him, her hand on her hip. "Well, if that's how you're going to play it, you can take me out to breakfast and pick up the check, too."

He draped his arm over her shoulder, and they continued down the hall. "Was planning on it."

"Hey, you two."

Stella tried not to cringe at the sound of Karen's voice. It was one thing for them to speculate that she might have spent the night with their son on Thursday night. But as he hadn't come home again last night and they were together at the hospital early in the morning, there was no doubt where they'd slept—with one another.

"Owen, are your parents fine with…"

"With what?"

"You know…us sleeping together."

He chuckled deeply. "Are you kidding? My mom phoned me with the safe sex talk that I've had every year since I was fourteen. And are you blushing? I gather your parents wouldn't take so kindly to the fact their little girl was in my dangerous clutches last night?"

"Of course I'm not blushing." Was she? "It's just, I don't appreciate everyone knowing my very personal business."

"Spoken like an only child."

Karen greeted her with a warm hug, as did Owen's dad. A family of huggers. *Great.*

"How's Charlotte?" Karen asked.

Yes! A safe topic that was in her wheelhouse. "She had a good night. Responded well to the extra saline and is now resting comfortably."

"What a relief. And how was the Market Gardens? As gorgeous as everyone says?"

"I, uh…"

Roger patted his wife's hand. "Honey, you're embarrassing sweet Stella here."

Sweet? Driven, yes. Overachiever. Single-minded. But never sweet.

Karen elbowed her husband in the side. "Oh, it's not as if I asked how comfortable the beds were." Then she leaned in. "How comfortable are the beds? We do have an anniversary coming up and—"

"Mom."

"Sorry, my dear." But a twinkle settled in Karen's hazel eyes. The woman wasn't the least bit sorry, and Stella suspected Owen's mother knew exactly what she was doing. What had Owen called her? A tormentor like his sisters? It was kind of sweet, really. As if she was welcoming Stella into the family.

Her mouth gaped. Welcoming her into the family? "Uh, I'm sure Charlotte would love to see you."

"Oh, yes. Catch you two later."

Stella watched as his parents entered Charlotte's room.

"That's one way to get them out of your hair. I'm impressed," Owen said. He tucked her arm through his. "Nice to have someone run interference. So I take it your parents are not so *involved* in your life?" he asked as they walked down the corridor toward the bank of elevators.

"Oh, I know they love me. They always made that clear. But we don't have the same kind of relationship you have with your family."

The bell above the right elevator dinged, and they stepped toward it at the same time. Even led off on the same foot. In fact, she was on his left side. As if they were still handcuffed together. The door swished open and they stepped inside and rotated to face the door. Still together. Still in unison.

"My parents value personal space. Alone time. It's not any better or worse than other people's families. Just different. In fact, my parents were very supportive when I told them I wanted to follow them into medicine. They helped me by stressing the importance of detachment and not getting too involved."

"But why?"

"If a doctor gives too much of herself, she'll be burned out in a couple of years. When she invests too deeply in someone else, it clouds her judgment."

Like now. Her shoulders slumped against the wall of the elevator. She was far from detached where Owen was concerned. He'd be leaving in a few days, and then where would she be?

"So you just become emotionless? A robot?"

"Just less like you. I mean, your emotions are crazy all over the place. No offense," she teased.

Owen towered above her and kissed her, a gentle caress of his mouth against hers. How could just that make everything inside her leap and seek more, more, more of him? "Crazy all over the place for you," he told her.

Then the elevator dinged. They'd reached the lobby, and Owen lifted his lips from hers. As they left the elevator, Stella moved to his right instead of his left.

Owen drove her to a restaurant a little outside of town. At one time it must have been a farmhouse. In fact, she spotted cows in the distance and a chicken coop. Sprigs of winter wheat waved in the breeze. Now a large sign posted above the door proudly announced Anton's Place.

"You won't get better pancakes than here. The flour comes right from the wheat grown on the farm, and the butter and cream are made here, too. Man, I forgot how much I missed this place," he said as they stepped inside and he inhaled. A tinkling bell above the door signaled their arrival, and the torturing scents of baking biscuits and strawberry preserves filled the air.

"Do you mind seating us near an outlet?" she asked the hostess.

After they were seated, Stella dug into her purse and pulled out a wall charger. "Since I still don't know where my car is, and that's my only other way to charge my phone."

"Minivan." His eyes crinkled at the corners. She'd be in some real trouble here if he ever decided to drag out the charm again.

"I prefer to think of it as a car. Since I still don't know where my *car* is, I grabbed the charger from my apartment. My plan was to plug in my phone at the hospital, but then I got distracted." By hazel eyes. A tempting smile. And a tight as— Never mind.

After she plugged in her phone, Owen handed her a menu. "Order whatever you want."

"That sounded a lot like a date," she teased.

"Nah. I just wanted you to know everything here is good. And since I'm paying, you can have whatever you want."

"Now it really sounds like a date."

Owen squeezed her hand. "Just go with it. What is that thing you say? Detach?"

After the waitress took their order, they fell into easy conversation. Owen's job sounded dangerous and exciting, and she caught a glimpse of why he was so intrigued by running into flames and fires to help, when most anyone else would be running away screaming. He wanted to hear about her life in Dallas, but she only shrugged.

"Up until yesterday when I woke up handcuffed to you, my life has been a series of classes and tests."

"So I'm the most exciting thing that's ever happened to you?" His hazel eyes twinkled.

"Don't get a big head."

Her phone buzzed and a smattering of texts and emails came into her phone. "Looks like the old girl is back in business," she said, swiping it from the table and scrolling through the data. Stella couldn't hide her frown. "Nothing from a lab, though. No texts. No emails."

"After we eat, we'll search the directory for every Pharmawhatever there is around here," he reassured her.

Damn, but the man could be sweet when he wanted to. "Wait. I have another idea." And she pulled up her recent telephone activity. "I think this is it. I called an unknown number on Friday." She gripped Owen's arm. "I made the phone call during our blackout time."

"Call it."

Stella pressed the Call Back button and then put the call on speaker so Owen could also hear.

"You have reached the offices of PharmaTest. Our offices are currently closed. Our office hours are Monday through Friday, nine a.m. to five p.m." Stella hung up without bothering to leave a message.

"You have your car keys with you?" he asked.

She nodded.

"I can drop you off to pick up your miniv—car after we eat."

Suddenly she wasn't sure she could keep any food in her stomach. "Thanks. That would be great."

Then they would go their separate ways. Her, to finish off the rest of her vacation doing nothing but laundry and catching up on her reading. Owen would finally have the weekend with the family that he'd driven to Texas for in the first place.

"So we have until Monday when the office reopens to get our answers," he said, his fingers drumming along the table.

"I thought you planned to head back to Colorado at the end of the weekend." Because the man had just dropped the words *we* and *Monday*.

He shook his head. "Called my chief. He gave me next week off. With the heavy rains a few days ago, fire season is officially over." Owen reached for her hand. "What do you say, Stella? Want to fill your week with me?"

9

LARISSA ESCAPED FROM Mitch's apartment on the pretext she had to pick up some clothes. Which was true, but she also had to find the two remaining subjects. This should have been a weekend of magic for her. She'd dreamed and pined and longed for nothing but the handsome doc for over a year, and now, when Larissa could finally hold him in her arms, stroke his amazing body and look into his eyes without fear of giving away her true feelings, she couldn't truly shake her anxiety about the rogue patients.

But when she got to PharmaTest, the beat-up yellow sedan and the red minivan were both gone.

Her stomach clenched. How could she have been so stupid? If she'd only waited here, Larissa would have spotted the owners. Could have talked to them. Gotten them to re-sign the liability clause all over again—now with the drug fully out of their system—and then all this would be behind her. No secrets or fears.

Just calm down. Larissa dragged a deep breath in, held the air deep in her lungs and then let it out slowly through her mouth. The cars were gone—that was a good sign, right? That meant the patients' memories hadn't been permanently wiped. They'd simply remembered where their cars were and driven them home.

Of course Dr. Durant would want to know why the drug hadn't been as effective for them, but it did stand to reason that if they hadn't needed to stay at the testing facility to sleep, then they'd missed other effects of the medication. They were fine.

Larissa keyed into the office just to be on the safe side. She'd left notes under the wipers of each car asking for the owners to contact her. It had been pretty windy last night, but maybe she'd lucked out.

But PharmaTest's voice mail remained empty. As Twelve and Ninety-Two had called in the wee hours of Friday morning, Larissa wasn't as worried about them. Still, subject thirty-five didn't live too far from her. Larissa could pop by her apartment, lay eyes on the woman and finally, *finally* put all her fears to rest.

MONDAY MORNING STELLA woke up to Owen's smile. For a moment, she indulged in imagining how wonderful it would be to wake up this exact same way every morning. Saturday he'd asked if she wanted to fill her week with him. *Hell* and *yes* had come to mind.

She'd protested when he reserved their suite for the week. "That place is far too expensive."

He'd only shrugged. "I live where I work. What else do I have to spend my money on?"

They'd spent the rest of Saturday and Sunday indulging in each other, leaving the hotel room only to visit with Charlotte or his family. The all-clear for Owen's gram came on Sunday morning, and they finally had the birthday party that had prompted Owen's trip in the first place.

"What do you think of getting away from this place overnight?" he asked on Tuesday.

"Not a four walls kind of guy, are you?"

He shook his head. "Nope. How about camping?"

"By camping, I'm picturing s'mores. Maybe flying a kite along the lakebed. Reading by candlelight?"

His brow furrowed, as if he was considering her ideas. "I was thinking along the lines of hiking through the woods and searching for the legendary goatman."

She rolled over and groaned into her pillow. The goatman was Lake Worth's resident monster. The stuff every child bravely told stories of during slumber parties and then feared when it was time to actually go to sleep. The goatman was right up there with Bigfoot and the chupacabra for frightening lore dating back decades. And Owen wanted to attempt to find the thing?

"Are you trying to get me intrigued by the idea of camping or make sure that I hate it?" she grumbled and reburied her face in the pillow. "Didn't you go tromping through the woods as a boy searching for it? Maybe along with a snipe hunt?"

"I thought it would appeal to your sense of science."

She perched up on her elbow and gave him a fierce smile. "Now that's just unfair." Because it was true. Now instead of dread, Stella now wondered if the thing actually existed and whether they would be able to spot any signs of it. How had he gotten to know her so well in so little time?

She rolled over onto her back and met his gorgeous eyes, more green this morning than brown. Wait, this was big. Owen wasn't just asking her to go on an adventure he'd probably trekked a million times before. No, Owen wanted to share a part of his life with her.

Stella wasn't sure she was ready for that. Then again, jumping in with both feet had so far been good for her. And Owen was going home to Colorado at the end of the week. Was it that much of a risk? She stretched lazily between the soft sheets, pulling the blanket down to reveal her tight-nippled breasts. Owen's gaze lowered, and she thrilled at how his eyes turned brown at the sight of her. Now instead of s'mores and kites or hikes and monsters she imagined making love by the fire. "Maybe we could invent a new game. Strip hiking? Whoever gets ahead has to lose an item of clothing."

He tapped his chin, pretending to consider it. "More fair if the person who falls behind has to take off something. It's a favor, really. Maybe it's the clothes slowing her or him down." His eyes crinkled in the corners. "I think I'm going to really love camping with you."

"Besides, now I can exorcise this making love against a tree fantasy I've had."

"*Had?* You've never wanted to go camping."

"It just came to me." She flung the covers off to the side. "C'mon, lazybones. Let's hit the trail."

BY TUESDAY MORNING, Larissa could no longer handle the guilt. The night before, she'd made love to Mitch with a quiet desperation. She'd wanted to blurt out her love, needed to, but held the words back.

She'd woken up this morning with her head on his chest, knowing it was probably for the last time. She had to confess.

He stretched beside her. "Good, you're awake. What if tonight we—"

"I lost four test patients on Thursday," she blurted.

Her beautiful doctor's eyes narrowed. "What?"

"Two of them showed up to PharmaTest yesterday. They're fine, and I'm pretty sure the other two are okay, too. I mean, there's nothing on the news and their cars are gone."

His hands clasped her shoulders. "You lost patients? How could this have happened? Why are you just now telling me about this?"

She wiped a tear from her cheek with her fingers. "It's the data…your work. I don't want it to be skewed."

His hands dropped to the bed.

"I know you'll never be able to forgive me for this."

He shook his head. "I'm trying to understand what happened on Thursday night. Where was the other lab tech?"

Her eyes narrowed in confusion. "There was no other lab tech. Just me."

Mitch scraped a hand over his face. "There are supposed to be three techs at the testing facility at all times. Or at least, I'm paying for three. Why didn't the security guard help you stop them?"

"Security guard?"

"You're telling me you were alone? All alone at the lab with dozens of subjects?"

She nodded, but she held back a sob. "I'm so sorry, Mitch."

He stroked her cheek with the back of his hand. "Larissa, I could forgive you most anything. I only wished you'd trusted me sooner."

She dragged in a shuddering breath. "There's more."

"More?"

"Those four patients…they didn't act like any of the other patients on HB121. Usually the subjects are lights-out until morning. Maybe a few sleepy hours of relaxation in the lounge before finally falling asleep. But these four, they were fully awake and ready to…"

"Ready to what?"

"Party."

This amazing man, the doctor who wanted to help

the world, sank his head in his hands. She touched his shoulder, but he flinched from her touch, and she let her fingers fall to the bed with a thump.

She swallowed and squared her shoulders. "I'm going to corporate today to explain. I'll make this right."

"Make sure you tell them how you were left alone. Those concerns must be addressed," he advised, his voice the cool professional once more. Mitch stood, grabbed his pants off the floor and dressed quickly in swift, jerky movements.

"Let yourself out," he said.

OWEN, IT SEEMED, was always prepared and ready for camping. He kept a two-person tent with all the supplies in a waterproof storage box in the bed of his truck. After a quick visit with his family and a stop at a camping goods store to buy her some sturdy boots, they headed to Lake Worth in search of trails and monsters.

The hiking trails were clearly marked and easy to navigate, and to her surprise, she actually enjoyed the exercise. It beat running in a circle around the indoor track at the fitness club any day. A light breeze cooled her sweaty temples, and she got to watch squirrels and cotton-tailed rabbits darting around—way better than the motivational posters she'd read thousands of times at the gym.

The typical central Texas scrub grass covered the area and trees lined their path, some still green while others had surrendered their color to fall. She and Owen hiked to the top of the bluff and held hands as they looked out over the lake.

He pointed to an area near the path. "This is where the infamous goatman has been spotted in the past."

On the drive from Dallas, she'd researched on her

phone for the signs of a sasquatch and recited them to him. "Do you see any unusual twig formations?"

They scanned the area. "Nope. Smell a strong odor?"

She took a deep breath then shook her head. "Only fresh air. Maybe a campfire."

"I think we'll be safe tonight. But don't worry, I'll protect you." There with the wind blowing through her hair and the fall sun on her face, Owen kissed her until she clung to him.

Afterward they walked hand in hand to the tree-heavy Greer Island, another popular goatman sighting spot, but they found nothing on the delightful island, which was connected to the banks of the lake by a small stretch of land.

Maybe it was the long walks or the fresh air or the lack of sleep over the past few nights, but by twilight Stella was fighting to hide her yawns, and they hadn't even set up camp yet.

"Ready to pop the tent?" he asked. He lifted his flashlight. "Monster hunting is especially fun at night."

"The only monster I want to see right now is the one in your pants."

With a chuckle, Owen grabbed her hand and they raced back to the truck. They drove a short distance to the isolated campgrounds he'd reserved online. Owen rushed through prepping the ground, showing her how to rake away the twigs and rocks so nothing would poke them through the bedcover and floor of the tent. With a few quick adjustments, the tent was popped and staked.

She slipped off her new boots and wiggled her toes while she watched as he built a fire in a ring. "Want to roast some marshmallows?" he asked, holding up a mesh bag filled with a box of graham crackers, chocolate and, of course, marshmallows.

Delight tingled inside her. He'd remembered her hankering for s'mores and sneaked in the supplies. But Stella wasn't hungry for food.

She gripped his wrist and dragged it into her lap. Then she circled lazy patterns on his arm. "I once read this book where the couple had sex against a tree. Did you forget I'd mentioned that?"

"The idea of it has been tormenting me." The firelight illuminated his smiling face, and his brow lifted. "But actually, I thought you were joking. Something to drive me crazy with. Being here with you brings a whole new dynamic to camping."

"Really? You've never had sex in the woods?"

He shook his head. "I've never brought anyone with me before."

She was humbled again by how this sexy and amazing man wanted to share his life with her. Stella lounged next to the fire, touched. But this trip wasn't supposed to be about emotional stuff. She launched herself into his arms. "Kiss me," she demanded and urged his lips to meet hers.

His head dipped and he possessed her mouth. Hot and forceful. In a motion she'd gotten used to making and loved, Stella looped her arms behind his neck and opened her mouth, taking ownership of his lips.

His fingertips traced on her skin, searing it.

"I've never wanted a man as much as I want you," she whispered into the tantalizing skin of his collarbone. His hand gripped her ass and hauled her against his body. The ridge of his growing erection pressed into her, thrilling her. She'd kissed playful Owen. And needy Owen. But never possessive Owen.

"You want that tree fantasy?" he asked.

She nodded, struck by the intense desire darkening his eyes as the fire cast beautiful shadows across his face.

Owen walked her backward until the bark pressed into her shoulder blades. "This tree looks like it will do the trick. No poison ivy. No roaming ants." He brushed his knuckles along her cheek. "Your skin is so delicate. I don't want to hurt your back against the bark."

"You'll figure out a way."

"Spread your legs," he instructed her. Then he stepped between her thighs, his cock now even more hard and demanding. The bulge in his jeans rubbed at the knot of nerves between her legs and she moaned.

He hissed in a breath. "I love the sounds you make. I could come just from hearing your sexy moans alone."

He palmed her breasts as he kissed and nibbled along her neck. Owen sucked her earlobe between his teeth and gently bit. Raw coursing need pierced through her, and Stella bucked up against him. She forced her breasts hard against his hands and demanded more friction between her legs.

His fingers sought the V of her T-shirt. He wrapped his fingers around the fabric and ripped. The sound of him physically tearing the clothes off her body made her knees shake and heat flood her vagina.

Owen kissed and licked his way down her torso. Her nipples puckered in anticipation of his mouth. Her head lolled against the tree trunk as he laved the heated peaks of her breasts with his tongue.

The bark poked at her skin, but Stella didn't care. All she wanted was the feel of his body—sweaty and hot against her, sliding inside her. Stella grabbed at his T-shirt. She couldn't rip the thing apart but she sure could shove it up and out of her way.

She tried to flatten her palms against his chest, but he eluded her caresses. "I want to touch you," she said, her voice heavy with need.

Owen stopped gently tugging at her nipple with his teeth long enough to drag his shirt over his head and fling it to the side. He reached for her hands, but instead of tangling his fingers with hers, he stretched her arms above her head.

"I want my hands on your body," she told him again. "All over."

Her firefighter shook his head. "It will go too fast. You turn me on too much."

He licked her neck while his hand weaved a slow, delicious path down her body. Owen stroked her breasts, drawing her nipples to fine, throbbing points. Then lower.

Owen smoothed his fingertips over her ribcage and circled her belly button. Then lower.

He cupped between her legs, and his thumb drove her crazy when he rotated it around her clit. Stella squeezed her eyes shut on a groan of pure pleasure and agony. He stroked her and her legs buckled.

She gripped him around the wrist to stop him. "You're going to make me come."

"And then I'll make you come again. Hands up," he ordered.

His voice was a sensual promise that left her no doubt he would back up his word with his body. He stroked her through her jeans until her muscles clenched and she ached to have him inside her.

But then his thumb moved away, and Stella gasped her disappointment. With a swipe of his tongue to her nipple, he worked to undo the button of her pants. His hand slipped inside, and a groan tore through her. The man hadn't even bothered to smooth her jeans down her legs. His impatience to touch her thrilled the hell out of her. She couldn't have stopped the smile that crossed her mouth if she'd wanted to.

"You make me feel so good." Her voice sounded heavy and aroused and slightly slurred.

"I'm about to make you feel a whole lot better." Then his finger slid under the wisp of lace that was her thong, and he fingered her clit without a barrier. Skin to skin.

A carnal ache twisted inside her. The man made her feel primal. Like a creature desperate to mate. She curved her hips to give him better access to her body.

His finger slid lower and into her slick heat. "You're so wet," he moaned against her neck. "Damn, Stella, you have no idea what that does to me. To know you want me just as much as I want you."

Stella thrust her hips forward to seek and graze against the heavy bulge in his pants. "Show me," she said. But Owen gripped her hips and spun her. He kissed the skin on her shoulders where the tree bark had rubbed against it. He lowered her jeans and she kicked them off and out of her way. The lacy panties fell next.

"Can't have your back scratched." He tapped her ankles with his hiking boot and she widened her stance. He stepped between her spread legs and tilted her hips to raise her backside higher. "I could stare at your beautiful ass all day." He kneaded and massaged her muscles until she felt loose and primed. Her legs began to quiver.

"You going to be able to stand?" he asked, his tone almost challenging.

Hell yeah, she would be able to stand. No way would she miss out on this experience with Owen. She leaned her weight against the trunk of the tree and arched her body toward him.

His anguished groan echoed through the trees. "The sight of you, open and ready for me. It's almost too much."

Stella wiggled her cheek against his cock. "Owen, I

need you now." And she was rewarded when he gripped her hips. Then he plunged, burying himself deep inside her. In one slow surge he filled her. When her legs trembled, his hands clutched around her waist to keep her stance firm, steadying to hold her in place.

His warm breath tickled along her neck, and then his teeth found her earlobe again. "Touch yourself, Stella. I wand to see you slide your fingers along your clit. I want to hear you moan as we both make you come."

She'd never stroked herself for her own pleasure while a lover pounded into her from behind. The thought of it, the anticipation of it, excited her. Stella bent her left elbow to bear more of her weight and leaned her forehead against her arm. She pinched her nipples lightly, then with more force, exactly the way she liked. Then she sank her fingers between her legs, around her pleasure center that longed for touch.

She grazed the sensitive skin and sucked in a breath at the exquisite sensation. What they were both doing to her body felt good. Better than good. Amazing. She was in charge of her own orgasm and could set the pace and the timing and she wanted to come *right now*. Her movements grew faster. Harder.

"Yes, Stella. Like that," he breathed into her neck.

She increased her speed.

"You're clamping around my cock, and it's driving me crazy. Yes. Just like that, darlin'. Exactly like that."

His rugged request sent her over the edge. She rubbed until every sensation built and tightened until she couldn't hold out anymore.

Her moan rent through the wilderness around them. In the bushes, an animal scurried away. And Stella became a creature of the night.

Owen's thrusts grew wild, more powerful. He leaned

more of his weight along her back. His body shook with the force of his control. He pumped inside her, his movements frantic. Then he groaned deep in his throat and she reveled in the guttural, needy sound.

She would wrap the memory of this moment around her like a warm blanket on a cool winter day.

After his last ragged thrust, Owen sagged against her. "That was amazing. You're amazing."

She smiled even though he couldn't see her.

"But, darlin', that sucked all the energy out of me. I don't mind falling on my face, but I don't want to take you down with me."

She nodded but could utter only one word. "Tent."

Stella shook as he carefully pulled out from her body. Another quaver shivered down her back. Their physical link broke, but she'd never felt so connected with another living soul.

She heard the sound of fabric rustling as he pulled on his jeans. Then Owen Perkins lifted her up and over his shoulder firefighter-style like he'd always threatened.

He set her down on her feet at the entrance of the tent. Stella fell to her knees and crawled through the opening. Owen zippered it shut behind them. She had the strength only to secure her unruly hair behind her head before she crawled into the sleeping bag.

Owen fell beside her, hauling her satisfied body onto his chest. She snuggled into his side. There was nowhere else she'd rather have been.

Her fingers found the scar on his ribs. "How'd this happen?"

His fingers tightened over hers, stilling her movement. Then the tension eased from his body. "I had another sister."

"Lily," she supplied, so he wouldn't have to recount every painful detail.

His gaze focused high above her head. "I dropped out of college after she died. I was angry and stupid. Mad at everyone. I didn't care if I lived or died. That's when I got into extreme sports. If you'd even call it sports. More like extreme feats of crazy."

She'd always sensed his adventure-seeking reckless spirit and shied away from it. Or at least tried to shy away. Stella waited for him to tell her the rest in his own way.

"I'd gone off for the weekend with a bunch of guys," he continued after a few moments. "We were bungee jumping off the bridge over the Red River. Not exactly legal and stupid dangerous because the cords were home-made."

Do not react. Don't.

"That night we decided to try our luck at walking across hot coals."

Her stomach hollowed for a moment. "And you got burned."

"And set one of the tents on fire. The local fire department came out." He rubbed at his neck. "I think the chief wanted to physically knock some sense into me. He called me an idiot, which I was, and told me if I wanted to kill myself I should do it without involving others." He smiled at the memory.

She heard the admiration in his voice. "Is that why you became a firefighter?"

"So I could call other people idiots? Absolutely."

She laughed.

"The next semester I went back to school, started volunteering with the medical studies and bought my first notebook so I could write on the side. It helped..." He took a deep breath. "It made losing Lily not so hard. A week after graduation, I moved to Colorado and began my training. And that, lovely lady, is my story." His voice had grown light, despite the weight of his words. And what he must be feeling.

She knew all his secrets now. "Thank you for telling me."

He only hugged her closer.

Her eyelids drifted shut as she toyed with the light dusting of hair across his chest she always found so fascinating.

She mumbled, "I love you," as sleep claimed her.

STELLA WOKE WITH a start. Had she confessed to Owen that she loved him last night? She covered her mouth to mask her gasp. Yes. She'd told him. Loud and clear.

She hugged the sleeping bag tight against her naked breasts. Outside the wind gently breezed against the canvas of the tent and a bird sang a sweet morning tune. And was that…she strained to hear. Yes, outside, Owen whistled. Stella squeezed her eyes shut.

She'd told him she loved him. Now the big question: Had she meant it? It was crazy. Stella had never even thought about her feelings for Owen—too caught up in the mystery of their meeting and her undeniable desire for him that never seemed to wane. Not once had any rational or cogent consideration of *hey, I'm in love with this man* ever crossed her mind.

What was wrong with her? Where was the in-depth analysis? The carefully planned steps? Detachment? Replacing emotion? *What? The? Hell?*

No, instead she'd just blurted out the truth.

And her love for him was the truth. She realized that now. But when? How? People didn't fall in love in a handful of days. Well, her kind of person did, apparently.

Love was supposed to develop between two people over time and with careful understanding. That's how it had been for her parents. Love didn't fuse together two people or blast through every problem like a supernova. Because bright bursts of energy fizzled out quickly. Always. It was science. She might love Owen now, but it wasn't a love she could trust. That either of them could trust. This connection between them wasn't long-term love. It couldn't be.

They were in the attraction phase of relationship-development theory. The hormone-induced giddiness of that phase was when all the long-term mistakes could happen. People wanted the affection to mean more so they *made* it mean more, not because it did.

The zipper on the front flap of the tent zipped open. Owen popped his head between the flaps, looking tempting and gorgeous and like everything she wanted in a man. He smiled when he realized that she was awake, and her breath caught in her throat.

Maybe he hadn't heard her last night. Maybe he was already asleep. Maybe h—

"So you love me, huh?"

So much for that futile wish.

He slid into the tent beside her. He propped his head on his hand and stared down into her face. His hazel eyes blazed, and then he dropped a quick kiss on her lips. "I love you, too."

The emotion his simple words triggered almost floored her.

She went through the motions of helping him decamp and sat silently in the truck on the way back to Dallas. The question *What am I going to do?* pounded through her mind over and over again. She couldn't even fall back on her always reliable detachment technique. Her emotions overflowed.

And all she could hear was her parents' advice. Love ruined plans. Emotion blew common sense out of the water. Feelings took everything away.

Beside her, Owen hummed or whistled or rubbed his hands along her thigh. No sign at all of any inner turmoil.

In some vain attempt at getting her mind off Owen and how she could no longer divorce herself from life, she dragged out her phone. Three missed calls? One yesterday and two today.

There'd been zero cell reception in the woods, so to save battery life she'd just turned the phone off. There were also three voice mails, all from the same number. PharmaTest.

She clutched the phone tightly in her hand. Checking her messages was a delaying technique, sure, a way not to have the conversation with Owen she dreaded. With relief she listened to the first message.

FORTY-FIVE MINUTES AFTER Larissa was fired—effective immediately—subjects twelve and ninety-two had walked through the door. Too little and way too late.

Larissa grabbed the picture of her rescue dog, Sadie, and stuffed it into the cardboard box on the floor.

"What's going on here?"

Larissa's hand stopped, suspended over the middle drawer of her desk. Great, Mitch was here—the perfect topper to the delicious cake of unemployment with humiliation frosting now on her plate. She squared her shoulders and forced herself to focus on the pens and pencils on her desk rather than look up and face Mitch. No, not Mitch. Dr. Durant. That's all he could be to her now.

The security guard cleared his throat, and Larissa

sighed and returned to the task of packing up the things she'd accumulated over the past three years of working at PharmaTest. "I'm leaving," she told the doctor, still not able to meet his gaze.

"You've been fired?" he asked, his voice raised. Incredulous. Angry.

That's when she made the mistake of looking him in the eye. Concern laced those dark brown depths of his. The man was gorgeous. How had she been able to keep her hands to herself these past three years? She'd seen him with a single-minded focus on his work, intensely absorbed on giving her the most amazing pleasure, and now concerned and outraged. For her.

Her shoulders drooped. "The exact wording was, 'We have opted not to renew your contract.'"

"They fired you because you raised your concerns. Larissa—"

She angled her head toward the security guard, then went back to her packing. "I'd rather not have this conversation right now."

"This is ridiculous," Mitch, er, Dr. Durant said as he reached into his pocket and fished out his phone. "I'm calling the head office right now."

Larissa stretched so she could grasp the books on the shelf behind her desk and slid them into the cardboard box on the floor. "It's okay. It was time to move on anyway."

"It's not okay. It's—" He directed his attention to the security guard. "Do you have to hover over her like this?" Mitch asked him.

The man nodded. "It's my job to make sure Ms. Winston doesn't remove any property belonging to PharmaTest from the facility or commit any acts of sabotage."

Mitch's breath came out in a hiss. "Screw that. I'm

taking Ms. Winston to the conference room where we will talk in private."

"I can't allow—"

"He's just doing his job, Dr. Durant. I brought this on myself."

Mitch raised his hand, palm out, to the guard. "Five minutes. I'll leave the blinds open so you can verify Ms. Winston isn't stealing anything." His fingers then wrapped around her elbow and he drew her along the hallway toward the conference room. He rolled the wand so the blinds were fully open, then nodded to the guard and closed the door firmly. He rounded on her, his hands fisted at his sides. Angry. Ready to do battle on her behalf. She'd never loved him more.

"What the hell is going on? Why didn't you call me?" he asked.

"This isn't your mess to fix," she told him with a shrug.

"If they fired you because you dared to raise concerns about their practices—"

She shook her head. "They fired me for unprofessional conduct in the office. I had an inappropriate relationship with you, and somehow they found out."

He rolled his eyes. "Let me guess, a policy they brought up only after *you* raised your concerns."

"Something like that. But Mi—er, Dr. Durant, I lost four patients."

"Due to understaffing."

"But I didn't contact anyone right away."

"I'm not going to let them treat you this poorly. They're all too happy to take my lab's money—"

"I don't want you to do anything. If I'm being honest, I've been at this job too long. The only reason I stayed was because I got to spend time with you."

A beautiful possessiveness flared in his eyes, and she felt lonelier than she ever had in her life.

He reached for her hand, but she shook it off. If he touched her, drew her into his strong arms, kissed her, she'd be lost. She'd only give in and take the easy way out. "They actually did me a favor by letting me go."

A smile tugged at the corner of his sexy lower lip. "Good for you. There's the spirit. You'll get a better job now. One you'll really enjoy. What would you like to do?"

"That's just it. I'm thirty years old and have no idea what I want to be when I grow up. I've drifted from job to job. This is the longest I've ever stayed at any one place, and in a lot of ways it's been the worst."

Mitch's eyes narrowed.

"You were the only bright spot. For three years I've watched people with all kinds of dreams walk through the offices of PharmaTest, and I envied them. One of the lost patients, she's going to be a doctor. Another one grew up in a group home and now he's a documentary filmmaker. A really successful one. Remember that rare phenomenon of HB121, the clarity of thought? Seeing this last group of subjects take what they wanted from life, I got that clarity, too. I pursued what *I* really wanted—you."

And there was that sexy smile again.

"But there's a thing with clarity. Sometimes it shines a light on the things you don't want to face." She cupped his cheeks in her hand. "I didn't call you because I knew you would try to fix this for me."

His hand covered hers, warm and reassuring and everything she wanted. "Of course I would have. I love you. I'd spend the rest of my life fixing things for you."

"And that's one of the reasons I love you. You'd fix the whole world's troubles if you could." Larissa shook her head. "But that's the thing. I need to figure this out for myself. Fix my own problems."

He gripped her shoulders. "I love you. You love me. I don't want you to go it alone. I sure as hell don't want to face tomorrow and the day after that without you. That's what people in love do. They tackle their obstacles together. As one." He scrubbed a hand down his face. "This is not how I wanted to do this. I have a ring back in my apartment and—"

"A ring?" Her voice caught in her throat.

"I bought it the day after our first night together."

That had to be the most romantic thing she'd ever heard.

"You're sort of leaving me hanging out here, Larissa."

His tone was teasing, but she couldn't miss the hopeful glow in his eyes. Tension emanated from his body. She began to sway toward him and felt her resolve dissipating. Her throat tightened further, and she had a hard time swallowing.

His smile widened as he spotted her quiet surrender. "I'm ready to start that next phase of my life. With you. Please say yes," he whispered against her mouth. Then his lips settled on hers and she couldn't help responding. She loved this man. Wanted him beyond reason.

Larissa whirled away from the man she loved. She wrapped her arms around herself and squeezed her eyes shut. "And that would be so, so easy. But I know what would happen. I'd let you take over. Fix me as you fix the world. But this is something I have to do alone. Just so I know I can do it."

"That's a no, isn't it?" he asked. His voice was tight, controlled. She'd hurt him and she felt not only cruel but also stupid because who would turn away from this man?

Desperately she wanted to add a *for now*—that she

was saying no only for the moment—but that seemed callous. She had no right to ask him to wait on her while she figured out her life. So instead she nodded, not trusting her voice. Or her resolve.

"Take care, Larissa."

Then she heard him twist the handle on the door and stalk down the hall. Her shoulders shook as she cried silent tears. Then, after a few moments, Larissa wiped the wetness from her cheeks with the back of her hand, closed the conference room door behind her and finished her packing.

10

THE WARM RAYS of sunshine streaming through the windows of their suite woke Stella. She should take advantage of this little luxury. She couldn't imagine a near future where nature's clock would stir her. The scents of rich cedar wood and fresh air, the smells that were all Owen, filled her nose, and she breathed in deeper. How long she lay there in the circle of his arms breathing in his scent and listening to the reassuring *thump*, *thump*, *thump* of his heartbeat she didn't know. Or care. Right now she simply wanted to live in the moment.

She wasn't sure when he awoke, but one moment his breathing was deep and steady and the next more ragged.

"Stop thinking so hard and roll over on top of me," he said, his voice still thick with sleep and temptation.

Stella would enjoy nothing more than to solve all her worries and concerns and problems with sex. "How do you know I was deep in thought?"

He hugged her. The Perkins clan liked to hug. "Because I know you."

She rolled away from him. Flopped her feet to the floor. "It's been less than a week. You barely know me."

His sigh was heavy with resignation. "I guess now's the time to say what we've both been thinking."

She took a deep breath, then blurted out her worries before she could change her mind. Drag him under the covers with a kiss and make love to him instead of facing reality. "It's not real. This thing between us."

"It's not real," he echoed.

His hand curled around her shoulder and he gently tugged until she faced him. Tenderness and a little bit of sadness lingered in the dark depths of his eyes. "It's like what Gram said. People come in and out of your life, and you, Stella, *you* came in exactly when I needed you."

Some desperate twinge of regret and love twisted inside her, and for a moment she was tempted to tell him how wrong he was. To go all prickly and sexy and challenge the hell out of him. Instead she shook her head. "It's science, really. Nature's trick of getting us together so we humans keep the species going. But emotions get involved and they have a way of kicking you in the end. There's always a price. I need that tattooed on my forearm so I don't forget."

Owen flung back the covers and stalked over to the window, his gaze trained on something in the courtyard below. "What I said to you in the woods, I meant it. I do love you. But you're right, this is just…a week. What happened between us happened too fast. Too hard. It will burn out just as fast. I only ever want to remember you looking at me the way you do now. With love."

She shrugged her shoulders. "It's funny. I'm the last person ever to be guided by emotion, and yet here you are, cautioning me about it."

"You return to your clinicals in a few days, right? You probably want to get home and start preparing."

She recognized the brush-off. Had some tiny desperate

hope still lived inside her that they could still spend the next few days together? Stella blinked at him a few times. Took in a deep breath and released it slowly. "You're right," she told him. "I should go."

She swung her legs over the side of the bed again.

"Actually, I was thinking about getting a head start back to Colorado. You don't have to leave. The room is paid up until Saturday."

But Stella shook her head. "No. It's time I get back to reality. Like you said. I've got a ton of reading to do, anyway. Maybe this way you can get some of your money back on the room. I'm going to change." She raced to the bathroom, pausing only long enough to grab a change of clothes from her suitcase.

AFTER CONFIRMING HIS CHECKOUT, Owen paced in the bedroom, and when that did no good, he paced in the living area. He grabbed his duffel bag, yanked the zipper open and stuffed inside what he could find around their room of his scattered belongings.

Why was he so mad? This was what he wanted. No ties before. No ties now.

Five minutes later the bathroom door opened. Stella emerged in jeans and a T-shirt. She'd scraped all that gorgeous hair he loved to sink his fingers into back into a tight ponytail. He'd never wanted her more. His hands fisted at his sides. "If you have everything, I'll walk you to your car."

She shook her head. "You don't have to do that."

"I want to."

Needed to. Needed to put Stella in that minivan she insisted on calling a car and watch her drive away. From him.

They rode down the mirrored elevator in silence. The

doors slid open and the sound of rushing water from the indoor fountain and lilting piano music surrounded them. But Stella didn't stop to run her fingers through the water; she trekked across the lobby and out the large glass doors.

A valet rushed to greet them. "Shall I pull around your car?"

"We're parked in the courtesy lot," Owen told him. Stella kept marching alone to the parking lot. Once beside her van, she dug through her purse until she located her keys. With a click of the button, the large door on the side slid open.

She turned to him then, and he handed over her luggage. Their fingers touched, the heat searing him, but she yanked back her hand quickly. Stella tossed her suitcase on the long bench seat.

Owen handed her a folded note card, like the ones they'd discovered the morning they'd woken up together handcuffed and naked in the bathtub. Her face blanched, and she hesitated to take it from his fingers.

"What's this?" she asked.

"It's my address in Colorado and my number at the station. I'll always remember what you did for Gram." He swallowed. "And for me. If you ever need anything…if you're ever in trouble, all you have to do is call."

She nodded and finally took the note card, careful not to touch him again. "Take care, Owen." She stowed his note in her glove box along with forgotten receipts and what looked like four years of insurance verification papers.

"You, too, Stella." Owen watched as she walked around to the driver's side and slid behind the wheel. He stood in the parking lot and watched her drive away. He stalked to his truck, threw his duffel bag on the passenger side, lunged into the cab and drove away before he could slam the car into Reverse, follow Stella to her apartment and try to convince her that they deserved more.

Thirty minutes later he was ringing the doorbell of Gram's house so he could say goodbye and get an early start on his trip home to Colorado. But only Bethany was in the house. His parents had taken his grandmother to a follow-up visit with her new primary-care doctor.

"Where's Stella?" Bethany asked when he found her doing laundry for Gram. She looked behind his shoulder.

"It's over. She's gone."

His sister nodded, then measured out the detergent and added it to the wash. "Yeah, you two seemed pretty in sync. Like you really cared about one another. She might even have been *the one*, so I figured she wouldn't be around long."

He blanched at her words. "What's that supposed to mean? Bethany, I can't make her want me."

"But you didn't even fight for her, did you?"

"Stella didn't seem too upset to see the back end of me."

"Maybe because both of you are too scared."

"What do I have to be afraid of?"

She screwed on the lid of the detergent and returned it to the rack where Gram stored her soaps and cleaners. "That she'll make you feel again. That maybe you will love her and she'll get sick or hurt or even die."

"I told her I love her. Does that make it better?"

"No, it makes it worse. Because I believe you really do love Stella and you'd rather see her walk out of your life now so that you won't love her more."

His hand sliced through the air. "I don't need your psychobabble. It was nice for a while, but now everything is righting itself again."

"It's not your fault." She flipped off the light and side-stepped around him to walk into the kitchen.

"What?" he asked, following her through the dark-ened hallway.

"Lily. It's not your fault she died."

Something squeezed tight inside him like a vise. He pivoted on his heel and aimed for the front door. "Tell everyone I said bye."

"There you go again, doing what you do best—running away from life and what you really want."

"I didn't run away to Colorado. I built a life there." And Stella and his family and everything here at home… it threatened that life. Stella wasn't what he wanted. He didn't want his family always hovering nearby. He cer-tainly didn't want his sisters barging into his life asking questions.

But mostly Stella. Forcing him to feel. *Isn't it already too late?*

Owen rubbed the back of his neck. "You really think now is the time? Really, now?"

Bethany only nodded. "Of course. It's the perfect time since you're already hurt and bleeding. Maybe a few truths will sink in before a new scab forms. I want you to really listen to me. You. Couldn't. Save. Lily." She poked him in the chest with each word.

His hand wrapped around her finger. "It was my bone marrow, Bethany. *Mine.* We were a damn near perfect match, and I still couldn't save her."

"And she was my sister, and we didn't match at all, and I couldn't save her, either."

"That's different."

"Why? Because you're the savior of the world so it's somehow worse for you than anyone else in this family that she died?" She yanked her finger from his hand and poked him in the chest again. "It's time you became part of this family again. I can't believe we let you do this to yourself for this long anyway. Well, no more, baby bro. The pity train ends now."

He'd stayed in Texas longer than he'd planned. He'd reconnected with his family. He'd done his duty.

Now it was time to go home. There was always something to clean at the station. A new piece of equipment or technique to learn. Without a word he wheeled around, stormed through the house, yanked open the front door and slammed it shut behind him. He stabbed his key into the ignition, then slumped against the seat. He'd get in a wreck if he drove right now in this agitated state.

His gaze snagged on one of the note cards from the Market Gardens hotel. Had Stella left him a note? His throat tightened and he grabbed the piece of paper like a lifeline and opened it. But it wasn't a note from Stella. In fact, he sat there confronted by his own handwriting.

Whatever you do, don't let Stella go without giving it a shot.

He stared at the words he must have written to himself only a few days ago. Thursday night. The ones he'd written under the influence of a drug that Larissa had told them may or may not give them clarity of thought.

Whatever you do...

This had been a warning to himself. For his eyes only.

...don't let Stella go.

Stella was the catalyst, but he was also here in Dallas. With his family. Maybe his note also meant *Don't let go.*

Owen shut off the motor of the truck. After grabbing his duffel bag and locking his truck, he shoved his keys into his pocket and walked back to the front door.

11

LARISSA RUBBED HER now completely sweaty palms on her black pencil skirt.

"Classy," she mumbled.

Someone walked past her and flashed her an odd look. Yeah, nothing to see here—just a woman talking to herself.

She'd been standing outside the medical facility for the past fifteen minutes working up the nerve to step inside. Perspiration beaded on her forehead.

She could blame her sweaty state on the late spring sun shining above her head, but she knew it was nerves. And fear of rejection. And the very deserved and dire thought of having to start all over again.

After several long months, she was ready to face the man she loved beyond reason. This time *she'd* be the one proposing. After all, she was the one who'd left him. She took a deep breath, squared her shoulders and opened the front door, sweaty palms and all.

A friendly receptionist greeted her when she entered, and directed her to Dr. Durant's floor. But the receptionist cautioned she wouldn't be able to enter the offices without an escort.

Okay, she'd just wait for someone to come out, Larissa decided. She glanced down at her watch. It was only forty-five minutes until lunch. Surely someone would leave the lab and she could pop through the open door. As a plan, it was terrible, but for some reason the element of surprise had felt like a good idea this morning when she'd formulated it. With advance warning, Mitch would have time to come up with half a dozen excuses not to meet with her.

At least with the stealth approach she'd have the chance to apologize for her behavior and be able to give him the gifts she carried in her bag.

Her plan to discreetly wait outside the door vanished when the elevator slid open on Mitch's floor and she spotted the large double-paned windows of the lab. Half a dozen white-coated doctors and assistants were working at long tables piled with cutting-edge medical research tools.

A card swipe as well as a phone on the side of the door guarded the lab from the unwanted. Otherwise known as people like her. But one of the doctors looked up just as she eyed the elevator button and lifted an arm in a friendly wave. There went her chance of sneaking out of here.

The doctor beside the first glanced up and smiled. Then the friendly doc pointed to the phone on the wall and pantomimed picking up the receiver.

Larissa shook her head and mouthed *It's okay* as she backed up toward the elevator and escape. Hopeful plans devised in the morning were stupid anyway. She'd simply call Mitch tonight and ask to meet him somewhere public like a normal person.

But just then Mitch came out of an office and asked a question of his colleagues. The pair pointed toward her.

She met Mitch's dark gaze through the glass. His lips parted and he flinched.

Regret and guilt slammed into her. She'd made him feel like that. Just seeing her made him physically wince. Man, she sucked.

Mitch turned to say something to his coworkers and for one really horrible moment, she thought he wouldn't buzz her inside the lab. Okay, so she might deserve to be left hanging.

But then Mitch pivoted on his heel and strode to the door. Relief made her shoulders sag, but then her stomach started to roil and churn with worry.

There was a buzzing sound followed by the snick of the door opening and then Mitch was beside her, gorgeous and cold, his dark eyes intense with some kind of banked emotion behind his glasses.

More people came out from the offices into the lab to not-so-discreetly watch Mitch on the other side of the glass. "I guess you don't get a lot of visitors up here, huh?"

Mitch shook his head. "What are you doing here, Larissa?"

His abrupt question shook her and she stiffened. But then, why should she be surprised? He wanted her out of there as quickly as possible, and she couldn't blame him.

"I'm back. Back in Dallas, that is, and man, is it hot here. Although not in here, this building. It's nice in here. You know, with the air conditioning." Babbling? Now? She'd practiced a speech. Had written down talking points. *Take a deep breath and try it again.* "I'm glad to see everyone still working on HB121. Did you ever find out the problem with the batch?"

Mitch lifted his glasses and rubbed at the bridge of his nose. "It was a mixing error at the manufacturer." Then he slid his glasses into place again and met her gaze. Emotion no longer lingered there. His face was a blank slate. "I have to get back to work."

"Okay, I understand. Do you have a break coming up? Maybe I could buy you some coffee."

"I don't think so, Larissa." He turned toward the door, already pulling out his security ID card from the lanyard he wore around his neck.

"Wait. Before you go. I brought you something. Actually three somethings. One for every year we've known each other." She pulled out the first gift-wrapped package from a paper bag and handed it to him.

Mitch stopped and faced her, eyeing the package she'd given him, his face still blank. "You don't need to give me anything."

"This was important." She nodded toward the present, afraid he'd try to give it back to her. "Please open it."

His dark gaze searched hers for a moment, and then he sighed and began to tear away the brightly colored paper. She'd never thought he'd be the kind to rip open a gift. She'd assumed he'd be more deliberate, like he was in bed. A tiny shiver rippled down her spine. She'd missed his lovemaking so much.

Maybe his haste was proof of how quickly he wanted her gone.

He tore away the last piece of gift wrap to reveal a small plastic lion with a wild orange mane and fierce teeth. He stroked the body of the animal with his thumb. "Am I missing something? I'm at a complete loss."

Larissa cleared her throat. "All over the world, the lion is a symbol of courage. Of never being afraid. When I walked out on you months ago, I thought I was being brave. Fixing my problems on my own was important, yes, but I was also afraid of what would happen if we stayed together. How long before you started wondering what you were doing with me? By then I was so in love with you, the idea of you leaving me scared the hell out of me. Ending it then was a whole lot safer. But I'm not going to play it safe anymore. Not with you. If you, uh, don't want to be with me, it won't be because I didn't try."

Mitch opened his mouth to say something, but she reached into her bag and pulled out the second gift, this time stuffed in a bag decorated with tiny stethoscopes.

He tucked the lion into the pocket of his white lab coat and then took the bag from her fingers, narrowly missing touching her. If he touched her now... Mitch buried his hand into the tissue paper only to pull out a single sheaf of paper. His eyes narrowed. "This looks like a bubble sheet you fill out for a test."

She nodded, unable to keep the smile from her face. "It is. In January I took a math placement test, the first step on enrolling, or re-enrolling, in college. I just finished my first semester because I realized what I want to be when I grow up. Finally."

He folded the sheet in half and handed it back to her. "Don't leave me in suspense."

"I'm going to be a high school counselor. I've talked to hundreds of people who've come through the doors of PharmaTest, some of them barely out of school, who needed a little direction. I've spoken with some of those subjects into the small hours of the night, and that was my favorite part of the job. Turns out, I'm actually kind of good at it. The money will be lousy, and the job is at the whim of tenuous school budgets, but now that I've figured out what I want, I can't imagine doing anything else."

"I'm happy for you," Mitch told her. His voice was warm, and she knew he really meant it. But his attitude toward her still remained chilly.

She'd hurt him badly. The kind of hurt that never really went away.

Everything hinged on her last gift. Larissa reached into the bag and pulled it out—this one was wrapped in fabric with a bow. She dropped the now empty paper sack on the floor beside her feet.

"The gift is inside the fabric, but it's wrapped in a quilt square my grandmother made. She never finished the quilt."

Mitch tugged at the bow and released the tie. Then he unrolled the fabric to reveal an old pocket watch. The watch wasn't expensive. In fact, the gold plate was worn in some places, and it had stopped ticking years ago.

"It was my grandfather's," she told him.

Lines puckered Mitch's brow and he shook his head. "I can't take something like this. It belongs with your family."

But she wrapped her hands around his, closing his fingers around the watch and quilt square that were so very dear to her. "I want you to have it. It's kind of like my pledge to you. That I'll never waste another minute of time that I could have with you."

He sucked in a breath, and Larissa realized that although she'd planned this grand gesture in hopes that he'd forgive her shabby treatment of him and maybe continue to date her, it wasn't until this moment that she'd told him that she wanted him. That she wanted to be with him.

Now she couldn't stop the words. "Dr. Mitch Durant, I am in love with you. I've been in love with you for three years." She shook her head. "No, for three years I was in love with the *idea* of you. Then I got to know the real you. The man here—" she splayed her hand across his heart "—and the reality of that man is so much better. I have enough college credits to cover my freshman year. So that leaves me with three years of school." Larissa took a deep breath, then met his dark gaze. "Can you wait for me for three years?"

His breath came out in a rush, and he began to smile. "I'd wait for you for forever."

She flung her arms around his neck and his lips crushed down on hers. A muted cheer rang out from behind the lab windows. His shoulders began to shake and she laughed right along with him, so filled with love and relief and tenderness for this amazing man who was going to be hers.

Mitch pulled away and rested his forehead against hers. "But I was thinking. Since we've already waited three years, couldn't that count as time served?"

"What do you mean?"

"It's not as if no one in the history of college has ever been married. Married people do get their education."

"Are you asking me to marry you, Mitch Durant?"

He angled his head toward the glass. "There are going to be a lot of disappointed people in my lab if I don't."

"There will be one very disappointed person in front of you if you don't," she confessed.

His fingers twined through hers. "Let's get out of here. A proposal is something I want to be just between us."

She tugged at his arm. "Wait, if you're not ready. Marriage is a big step and—"

He cupped her face between his hands, his brown eyes warm and filled with love. For her. "Larissa, I bought the ring the day after we loved each other in the lab. Remember?"

The morning they'd played doctor in the offices of PharmaTest. The memory of that still gave her shivers of pleasure.

"What shall we play this time?" she asked.

"How about two people who got exactly what they wanted?"

THREE WEEKS AFTER tackling the first of the summer wildfires, Owen's colleague Callie cornered him in the equipment room where he was busying himself checking the dates of the MREs. She'd only just returned from her winter job, and this was the first time they'd had a chance to talk. "What happened in Texas? I know you weren't looking forward to it."

Owen only shrugged. "Nothing."

"It's just that since you've been back, you've been kind of a dick."

"You just got here," he pointed out, moving on to check the state of the parachutes.

"The guys warned me ahead of time, even though they were too chickenshit to say anything to you themselves. Apparently, there's just some weird bro code that says they have to keep their mouths shut. Lucky for you, I'm not bound by that." She flashed him a half smile.

Owen dropped the parachute pack. "You're supposed to say, 'No offense.'"

Callie's brow wrinkled. "Huh?"

"Before you insult someone, you're supposed to say, 'No offense.' Then have at it."

"Is that some kind of weird Texas thing? I *meant* to offend you. You're being insufferable. So it has to be a woman."

His mouth dropped open. "How'd you— Never mind. I get it. You guessed and I just confirmed it."

"So what's the issue?"

"None of your business unless you have a way to fix it."

Callie lifted her hands and shrugged. "Just because I'm the girl in this conversation doesn't mean I'm the relationship expert. Although to be fair, most anyone can spot the problems in another person's life. Now spill."

"Thought you weren't the relationship expert."

"It's not for you I'm asking. It's for me. And the rest of the guys. Did I mention you're insufferable?"

Satisfied with the parachute, he examined the next one. "She's a doctor in Texas. I live here."

"Strange how they don't have fires in Texas. Or doctors in Colorado. So what's the problem? She doesn't love you back?" Callie asked.

Owen shook his head, then grabbed for another parachute. This conversation was distracting him. He'd have to double-check his work later. "She says she loves me, too. It's a lot more complicated than that."

"No, it's not. C'mon, man. Now you're just inventing problems. It's a dick move."

"Don't call me a dick."

"Then don't be one. The question you need to ask yourself is why. Why are you making this so hard? You're two people who clearly want to be together. Why aren't you?"

Yeah. Why wasn't he? He shoved the backpack at Callie, then charged out of the equipment room. Owen didn't stop until he stood outside, where the mountains framed the deep blue sky and the trees stood tall and green. He breathed in the clean, piney scent and wondered, for the thousandth time, if he'd ever get over Stella. Her smile. Her scent. Her love.

Things *had* changed since he'd returned from Texas. He no longer kept his family at a distance. His sisters had even taught Gram how to FaceTime, and they video chatted once a week. But when Gram mentioned Stella had popped by to see her, he'd made his excuses and severed the connection fast. He wasn't ready to talk about Stella with his family.

But that night, he dug up her phone number and called her. Stella hadn't answered. She'd probably been on some long late shift at the hospital. But he'd heard the inviting sound of her voice and had to squeeze his eyes shut. How had he been able to walk away so many months ago? Time was supposed to heal, but the ticking clock only made it worse.

That night he'd made a decision; Owen just had no idea how to make it happen.

The door he'd used to escape Callie's questions opened and closed with a *whack*. But he didn't turn around. Hadn't him leaving the equipment room been enough of a hint for Callie?

"I used to think emotion clouded a doctor's judgment and had no business in how I treated patients. Now I'm not so sure. Maybe a little investment will make me a better physician."

Stella.

He fisted his hands tight, then faced her. Her gorgeous, untamable hair hung in waves around her shoulders. She wore the hiking boots he'd bought her in Texas, shorts and a T-shirt, and she'd never looked more beautiful to him. He'd never wanted her more.

"After all, bedside manner is important. Studies show patients will share more information with a doctor they like. And sometimes, actually a lot of times, that can save a patient's life. It's all about trust. I made that realization because of you."

He shoved his hands in his pockets. "So is that why you're here? To thank me?"

Stella shook her head. "No, I'm not here to talk about my bedside manner or about getting involved with my patients."

"What are you here to talk about?"

Her gaze lowered to his lips, then back up to his eyes. "You."

In two long strides he stood at her side.

"I used to think if I got emotionally involved and invested I'd be done in a year. But you…you make me feel…"

"What?"

"Everything."

His body erupted in a slow burn. "That's good, right?"

She shook her head. "No, that's bad. Really, *really* bad. It causes chaos. Bedlam. Turmoil. But then I realized something while you were gone."

"What's that?"

"Relying on someone else doesn't make you weak." Stella took a deep breath, her dark-eyed gaze met his, and then she pressed onward. "I *want* to rely on you, Owen."

His body went rigid.

"You're not saying anything. I knew I shouldn't have listened to Bethany."

He reached for her wrist to prevent her from turning away and leaving him. "You talked to my sister?"

"Your whole family, really. Your mom's been making sure I eat on my long days at the hospital. Your gram's making a special tier in her garden with my favorite flowers. Roger is showing me how to build a proper campfire."

He smiled. His family already loved and accepted her,

though he knew their loud and overbearing natures over-whelmed her sometimes. "For all my family's craziness, I don't want to settle for less."

"Maybe throw in a few moments of quiet and you have yourself a deal?"

"And personal space," he added.

Stella sucked in her bottom lip for a moment. "Owen, I love you. I always will. Common sense and attachment theory would tell me that distance and time would lessen what I feel for you, but they haven't. I feel more."

He'd hungered for this woman, ached for her, and here she stood in front of him, like his every dream and wishful thought come alive. Stella dug around for something in her back pocket. "I also found this."

She handed him a notecard, like the ones they'd discovered scattered all over their suite at the Market Gardens.

In case you don't remember last night, let me just tell you that you are one lucky woman. Lucky because you get to discover all over again what a great kisser Owen is. In fact, he is everything you'd want in a man. Besides sexy as hell, he's adventurous, caring and clearly knows how to give you org—

She took an unsteady breath. "I knew. That first time I knew."

Reminded him of his own note he just hadn't been able to get rid of. "What do you think that last word is?"

The woman he loved, would always love, shoved at his shoulder. "Owen."

His hand curved around hers and then their fingers entwined. "Come with me."

"But—"

Owen led her around the station, their feet crunching on twigs and leaves as they trekked toward the parking lot.

"I'm glad this won't be wasted." Owen reached into the glove box of his truck and pulled out a small jeweler's case. He opened it to reveal a beautiful diamond ring.

She blinked up at him. "Wait, what? You already had this? You *knew* you were going to ask me to be with you all along while I stood there pouring out my heart like a sacrifice to the god of emotion?"

He frowned down at her. "You're really ruining my big romantic gesture."

A sexy smile lifted the corner of her mouth. "Yeah, I guess I am. Sorry."

Owen drew her into his arms. Stella rested her head against his chest. "Figured I might not see that emotional side of you for a while."

She laughed. "Or ever. But no, there's a freedom in sharing my heart with my man. Of leaning on you and knowing you will lean on me, too."

"So how about sharing the rest of your life with me?" he asked.

She nodded. "I love you, Owen."

"I'd fist pump if that weren't obnoxious." Then he slid the engagement ring onto her finger. "I love you, Stella. You are my life. And now my future."

She gazed down at the solitaire on her finger. "And you bought this ring even after…"

"You kicked me to the curb? Yeah. I knew after a few months without me I'd hear from you."

"Seriously? I completely underestimated your ego."

Owen lifted her chin and caressed her lips with his. "Actually it was more like wishful thinking. I bought it a few days ago. I was about to go find you. I wasn't going to last another week without you."

"Good thing I pursued you first."

Then she settled her lips on his.

* * * * *

COMING NEXT MONTH FROM

Available February 16, 2016

#883 HER SEXY MARINE VALENTINE
Uniformly Hot!
by Candace Havens

To get past Valentine's Day, new friends Brody Williams and Marigold McGuire are pretending they're in love. But their burning-hot chemistry means the Marine and the interior designer's make-believe is quickly becoming a super-sexy reality...

#884 COMPROMISING POSITIONS
The Wrong Bed
by Kate Hoffmann

One bed. Two owners. Sam Blackstone and Amelia Sheffield are willing to play dirty to get what they want. But at the end of the day, will that be the bed...or each other?

#885 SWEET SEDUCTION
by Daire St. Denis

When Daisy Sinclair finds out the man she spent the night with is her ex-husband's new lawyer, she flips. Is Jamie Forsythe in on helping steal her family bakery? Or was their sweet seduction the real thing?

#886 COWBOY STRONG
Wild Western Heat
by Kelli Ireland

Tyson Covington and Mackenzie Malone were rivals...with benefits. But when Ty is forced to put his future in Kenzie's hands, he has to do something more dangerous than loving the enemy: he has to trust her.

REQUEST YOUR FREE BOOKS!
2 FREE NOVELS PLUS 2 FREE GIFTS!

HARLEQUIN®

Blaze

red-hot reads!

SPECIAL EXCERPT FROM

❤ HARLEQUIN®

Blaze

*Daisy Sinclair is determined to get over the
embarrassment of Colin Forsythe accidentally
seeing her naked…something that he didn't seem
to mind at all!*

Read on for a sneak preview of
SWEET SEDUCTION
by New York Times *bestselling author*
Daire St. Denis

"Ms. Sinclair?"

Daisy looked up at the man standing in the doorway to her office. Yes, he was Colin Forsythe all right. His wavy brown hair might have been a bit longer than in the picture beside his column, but he had the same square jaw, the same nose—though in person it was a little crooked—and the same full lips. While he was recognizable, his byline picture did not do him justice. In that picture he came off as stern, albeit in a well-coiffed, intellectual sort of way. In person? Wow. He looked anything but. His eyes sparkled with irreverence, his lips turned up at one side as if he was trying to keep a sinful smile in check, and he was just…bigger. More like a professional athlete than a distinguished foodie.

His eyebrows rose under her appraisal. "Do I pass?"

Daisy cringed. Good-looking. Big ego. No surprise. Obviously, he was going to make this impossible for her. But he was Colin Forsythe, and she'd been anticipating this interview ever since taking over Nana Sin's bakery three years ago. Of course he had to show up today of all days.

"Can we pretend, for my sake, that we're meeting for the first time, right now? That you didn't just…" Daisy paused to take a deep, composing breath. "Hello, Mr. Forsythe." She walked around her desk, hand outstretched. "I'm Daisy Sinclair. Welcome to Nana Sin's."

He rubbed his jaw as if trying to massage his face into a serious expression. It didn't work. When she was close enough, he took her hand and shook it firmly. "It's Colin."

"Colin." She set her lips in a grim line and sauntered past, head held high. At the door she turned. "Shall we?"

"Shall we what?"

Daisy rolled her eyes. "Aren't you here to see the bakery?"

In one step Colin was beside her, looking down at her. Damn, the man was tall. Not fair. And what the hell was he doing, blasting her with that sinful smile of his?

"I've already seen everything." He grinned.

She groaned.

He came closer, spoke more softly. "What I'd really like is a taste."

The way he looked at her made Daisy think he wanted to taste her.

Don't miss
SWEET SEDUCTION
by Daire St. Denis,
available March 2016 wherever
Harlequin® Blaze® books and ebooks are sold.

www.Harlequin.com

Turn your love of reading into
rewards you'll love with

Harlequin My Rewards

Looking for more wealthy bachelors? Fear not!
Be sure to collect these sexy reads from
Harlequin® Presents and Harlequin® Desire!

A FORBIDDEN TEMPTATION
by Anne Mather

Jack Connolly isn't looking for a woman—
until he meets Grace Spencer! Trapped in a
fake relationship to safeguard her family,
Grace knows giving in to Jack would risk
everything she holds dear… But will she
surrender to the forbidden?

Available February 16, 2016

SNOWBOUND WITH THE BOSS
(Pregnant by the Boss)
by Maureen Child

When gaming tycoon Sean Ryan is
stranded with irascible, irresistible contractor
Kate Wells, the temptation to keep each other
warm proves overwhelming. Dealing with
unexpected feelings is hard enough, but what
about an unexpected pregnancy? They're
about to find out…

Available March 1, 2016

Love the Harlequin book you just read?

Your opinion matters.

Review this book on your favorite book site, review site, blog or your own social media properties and share your opinion with other readers!

Be sure to connect with us at:
Harlequin.com/Newsletters
Facebook.com/HarlequinBooks
Twitter.com/HarlequinBooks

THE WORLD IS BETTER
WITH
Romance

Harlequin has everything from contemporary, passionate and heartwarming to suspenseful and inspirational stories.

Whatever your mood,
we have a romance just for you!

Connect with us to find your next great read, special offers and more.

f /HarlequinBooks

🐦 @HarlequinBooks

www.HarlequinBlog.com

www.Harlequin.com/Newsletters

◆ HARLEQUIN®

A *Romance* FOR EVERY MOOD™

www.Harlequin.com